RANCHER'S BLOOD

Also by W. W. Lee

Rustler's Venom
Rogue's Gold

RANCHER'S BLOOD

W. W. Lee

Walker and Company
New York

First published in the United States of America in 1991
by Walker Publishing Company, Inc.

Published simultaneously in Canada by Thomas Allen & Son
Canada, Limited, Markham, Ontario

Library of Congress Cataloging-in-Publication Data
Lee, W. W. (Wendi W.)
Rancher's blood / W. W. Lee.
p.   cm.
ISBN 0-8027-4120-7
I. Title.
PS3562.E3663R36   1991   91-12858
813'.54—dc20   CIP

Printed in the United States of America

2   4   6   8   10   9   7   5   3   1

This is for Max Allan Collins,
for his generosity, support,
and friendship

CHAPTER 1

BIRCH kept an eye on the man at the bar. For the price of a bottle of rotgut and a silver dollar, the bartender had pointed out Clem Johnston, wanted for murdering a wealthy rancher back in Carson City. Trying to act casual, Birch poured another glass of whiskey. It was hard to believe that finding Johnston had been this easy.

So far, Johnston hadn't caught on to the fact that he was being watched, and Birch wasn't in a hurry to make the arrest until he was certain that this was the man he was looking for.

Three days ago, Tisdale had wired Birch about this job. Clem Johnston was accused of killing Frank Ashton. Johnston had been found standing over Ashton's body, the murder weapon in his hand. The dead man's son, John Ashton, had held Clem Johnston until the marshal arrived, but the ranch hand escaped custody and eluded the law for several weeks.

Finally, Johnston was spotted up Birch's way. At first, Birch wasn't sure about taking up bounty hunting again; he'd done plenty of that back in Texas as a Ranger, but it had never been a pleasant experience.

On the other hand, it was an easier way to make money than punching cattle. After deciding to take the job for Tisdale Investigations, Birch left his ranch job and headed for Pine Ridge in the Nevada Territory, where Johnston had last been spotted.

Johnston was now talking to the bartender. His hand hovered nervously near his gun. Birch noted with interest that Johnston wore his holster on the left side.

After less than a minute's exchange, Johnston inclined his

1

head toward the saloon keeper and looked up in the mirror toward Birch. He dug into his pocket, slapped some coins down on the bar surface, and slid them toward the bartender. Then he downed his drink and left quickly.

Birch glanced at the bartender as he followed Johnston out the door. The saloon keeper was covertly palming a silver coin and watching Birch from under hooded eyes. Birch wondered if Johnston had suspected that he was being followed, or if the bartender had just offered the information in the hopes of getting paid twice. It was no matter to Birch. He'd rather capture Johnston somewhere less crowded anyway.

Jefferson Birch settled into the saddle and pointed Cactus in the same direction Clem Johnston was headed—south. Just outside of town, the wanted man spurred his horse into a hard gallop. No longer able to silently shadow his quarry, Birch urged his horse Cactus into action, intent on capturing Clem Johnston.

It didn't take much effort on Cactus's part to match speed with Johnston's nag, and as Birch approached the desperado and his mount he slid his Sharps carbine out of its saddle boot. He didn't want any blood shed—especially his own—but if he had to shoot, a carbine gave him better odds of hitting the mark than his Navy Colt.

Johnston glanced back, a fearful look in his eyes, and tried to goad his old horse into outrunning the horse and rider behind him. Birch ducked out of reflex as he saw the desperate man draw his gun and shoot in his direction, widely missing the mark. He wondered if Johnston had deliberately missed or was just a bad shot. He didn't know too many southpaws who could shoot worth a damn.

On the verge of returning the shot, the ex-Ranger held back at the last moment. He had a feeling that Johnston was shooting to scare him, not to kill him; Birch had hoped that he could bring Johnston in without resorting to guns.

Somehow, Johnston got a little more speed out of his nag

just as they came to a bend in the terrain. Birch watched him disappear in a cloud of dust and urged Cactus to a breakneck gallop to catch up.

If Birch hadn't looked to his left as they came round the bend, he might have missed the riderless old horse, partially hidden by scrub brush and snorting heavily from the chase.

Pulling Cactus up short just beyond the brush, Birch slid down from his horse, his carbine swinging easily in his hand. He drew a sling from his saddlebags and slipped it on, then slid in his carbine. He wore the holster on his right side; it was cumbersome, but he could get at it if he needed to use it. His Navy Colt was in his hand, primed and ready.

Birch paused and listened. Boots striking and scrabbling up a hard surface sounded not too far off. He followed the racket, pausing every now and then to listen and make sure he was headed in the right direction.

When he reached the foot of a smooth stone rise, he stopped again. He knew Johnston was close, but it was hard to tell where the noise came from until a few pebbles rained down on his hat. He looked up in time to see a flash of boot heel disappear from view, heading upward.

Where is this fellow going? Birch asked himself as he searched for a way to ascend the bald rock. Off to the right behind some sagebrush, Birch found a narrow winding path with rough handholds spaced intermittently on the bare rock face. Shoving the Colt into its holster, Birch began the long ascent.

The climb seemed to take forever, and Birch began to wonder if Johnston had evaded him. Perhaps the wanted man had found another narrow path that doubled back and descended, leading him back to his horse and temporary freedom.

Birch was getting near the top of the bluff, but it was too quiet up there. Suddenly, a shot rang out. Instinct took over and Birch flattened himself against the smooth rock face.

His left foot scrabbled for a hold and he felt himself losing his grip.

"Don't come any closer, mister," Johnston shouted from above. "I may not have hit you that time, but I'll kill you if I have to." It was hard to think of that thin voice as belonging to a murderer—Clem Johnston sounded more like a boy than a man.

Birch wasn't much in the mood for talking while he was hanging by his fingernails from a narrow rocky ledge. He tightened his grip on the shallow handholds in the rock and found a tenuous hold for the toe of his right boot. Shifting his head from right to left, he saw a wider ledge a few feet away. Holding his breath and ignoring the warm sweat that trickled down his spine, Birch stretched one leg toward the ledge.

It was only when he'd pulled himself up onto the wider ledge that he was able to breathe again and focus on the problem of how to capture Clem Johnston. He didn't like the idea of trying to haul a dead body down this sheer rock face.

"I mean it," Clem Johnston shouted. "I ain't goin' back with you, mister, so you can just haul yourself back down this rock and head back to where you came from."

Birch relaxed against the warm rock surface and called, "I could starve you out, Johnston. All I have to do is camp near the foot of this bluff and you'll be down sooner or later." Trying to reason with the man on the ledge above him, Birch continued, "Why don't you give yourself up peacefully? I won't shoot you. I just want to take you back to Carson City for trial."

There was a pause. Birch was beginning to think he could convince Johnston to give up.

"Ain't comin' down, mister," Johnston said. "I'll stay up here till I die, if I have to. No sense in you staying here and getting killed." He fired his gun again in warning.

Birch sighed. This was going to be a tough one. For a wanted murderer, Clem Johnston was a bad shot. He'd had at least one clear opportunity to kill Birch, but had only fired a warning. Of course, Birch called to mind that the ranch owner whom Johnston was accused of killing had been stabbed, not shot.

"Okay, Johnston. You win. I'm going back to Carson City." Birch started to climb down.

Silence followed before Johnston, in a suspicious tone, called out, "How do I know you're really going? You could be waiting for me down at the foot of this rock."

Birch tried to sound as if he didn't care one way or another. "Have it your way. So I'll be waiting at the bottom of this rock for a measly one hundred dollars' reward. You can stay up there till you starve for all I care." He started down the grade; the descent should have been easier, but Birch found it difficult to keep from looking down.

"I just might do that," Johnston replied dubiously. "I have nothing to lose, you know."

Birch just grunted. He was having increasing trouble locating handholds on the sheer rock. The current one was giving him quite a bit of trouble. He finally found what felt like a handhold and clung to it, wishing that he didn't have the extra weight of the carbine; it hung at his side like a rigid papoose.

Birch shifted his weight to get into a more comfortable position, but his new handhold started crumbling and gave way. He fell swiftly, before he had time to call out his surprise. It was a short fall—instead of hitting the rocky ground as he'd expected, he landed in a sage scrub. After struggling to disentangle himself from the sagebrush that had softened his fall, Birch straightened up and made sure all his limbs were in working order. He'd have one hell of a bruise on his tailbone tomorrow morning.

From high above, he heard the anxious voice of Clem Johnston. "Mister? Hey, are you okay?"

Birch was on the verge of calling out when he realized what a good ruse this was. He'd just have to wait. Feeling guilty for pulling such a dirty trick, Birch settled down out of sight to wait. He was thirsty after his climb and his unceremonious descent, but he didn't want to risk going after the canteen on his saddle in case the wanted man caught a glimpse of him.

Birch didn't have long to wait. Clem Johnston scrambled down the steep bluff as if he'd been climbing rocks all his life. When he reached the ground, Johnston peered around, looking for Birch's broken body.

Birch stepped out from behind a large rock, his gun aimed at his quarry.

"I hope you're ready to go back with me," Birch said easily. "I'm sorry I had to get you down from there with a trick."

Johnston's shoulders seemed to cave in on themselves. He frowned, replying, "I should have known better . . ."

Birch smiled grimly and shook his head. "I really did slip, only the fall wasn't more than about ten feet. I landed in that sagebrush."

Clem Johnston handed over his gun. Birch clapped irons on him, and they mounted their horses for the long ride back to Carson City.

Birch studied his prisoner up close for the first time. Clem Johnston appeared to be in his early twenties, with a clean, square-cut chin and light blue eyes. His thatch of straw-colored hair, tanned face, and calloused hands were signs that he spent most of his days outdoors.

Johnston was a healthy-looking young man and Birch had an idea that he was popular with the ladies. But from the little contact that Birch had had with his prisoner, Johnston also appeared to be likable beneath his reticence. It was hard to picture this fresh-faced kid killing another man but, Birch thought, who was he to judge?

There was little talk as they headed for the town of Paradise Valley. Clem Johnston stared morosely ahead, ignoring Birch's attempts at conversation.

Birch finally fell silent and brooded over the wire that

Tisdale had sent three days ago. Tisdale had sent it from Carson City, but the gist of it was that he was going on to Paradise Valley to await word from Birch on the Clem Johnston matter. It was pure chance that Birch had caught Johnston about fifteen miles east of Paradise Valley.

What Birch couldn't figure out was why Tisdale would travel several hundred miles north to a small town on the chance that his investigator might catch a wanted murderer. It would have made more sense for Tisdale to wait in Carson City.

"Where we going?" Clem Johnston scowled at Birch, then took a quick look around the surrounding landscape. "This ain't the way to Pine Ridge."

"We're not going back there," Birch replied. "Pine Ridge isn't the best way back to Carson City. We're going to Paradise Valley, where you'll have a nice warm cell waiting for you. Then tomorrow, we head for Carson City."

"We're taking a stagecoach back?" Johnston sounded almost hopeful. "I never been on a stagecoach before."

"We'll see" was Birch's short reply.

The sun beat down hard and hot on the two men. In the distance, a range of mountains rose up to taunt Birch and Johnston with the promise of a cooler ride. But the peaks were all too far away for them. Birch guessed the distance to be about two days' travel time.

Paradise Valley was much closer. When they reached the little town, Birch would deposit Johnston in the local jail, then head straight to a hotel or rooming house and have someone draw a cool bath for him. He wanted to scrub away the grime from his long climb.

Tisdale would have to wait a little longer for their meeting.

CHAPTER 2

LOCKING up Clem Johnston proved to be more difficult than Birch had figured. The town of Paradise Valley was no more than a saloon, a hotel, a blacksmith shop, and a general store out in the middle of nowhere. Birch searched the single main street for a jail but, finally, his prisoner in tow, gave up and entered the saloon, intending to seek information.

The saloon was a small dark room with a short counter to the left of the door. There were two tables that looked like they'd seen numerous bar fights; a few rickety chairs were scattered around the room.

A scrawny old man sat at one of the tables, nursing a shot of whiskey. He wore too-big pants patched at the knee over a pair of sweat-stained long johns. A battered, shapeless hat was crammed on his head, and a fringe of white hair framed rheumy eyes and a bright red nose.

There wasn't anyone behind the bar, so Birch spoke to the old sot at the table. "Where can a stranger get some information around here?"

The man seemed to notice Birch and Johnston for the first time. His voice came out harsh, like he hadn't used it in a long time. "Sam'll be back tomorrow. I'm watching the place. For the price of a drink, I'll answer your questions. You and your friend there look like you could use a drink yourselves. Serve yourself and leave your coin on the counter. Five cents a shot."

Birch moved over to the counter to pay and pour three whiskeys. Despite the fact that Johnston was an accused killer, Birch liked the kid and was willing to stand him for a drink. "I'm looking for the law around here. You know where I can find him?" He handed the drunkard one of the shots.

The old man drained it in one gulp and set down the empty shot glass. Then he jabbed a thumb at his chest and said, "You're lookin' at him." Birch must have looked surprised because he added, "No one else wanted the job. Name's Higgins. Gabe Higgins."

"Glad to know you. You got a jail or holding place somewhere?"

The marshal's watery bloodshot eyes brightened. He indicated Clem Johnston with a nod of his head. "I noticed the young one don't speak up much. Maybe the cuffs got him all choked up."

Birch glanced at Johnston. Johnston, in turn, looked at Marshal Higgins, then tipped his whiskey glass back and swallowed. A moment later, Johnston's eyes widened and he gasped as the liquor took full effect.

"Good God! What is that stuff?" Clem Johnston sputtered, clutching his throat with his cuffed hands and trying to take a breath. It came out like more of a gasp.

Marshal Higgins chuckled and held out his own drained shot glass. "That, son, is called homemade rotgut. Want another? Might take the bite out of that first one."

"No thanks, mister," Johnston said, falling into a nearby seat, the chair legs creaking and wobbling with the sudden weight.

Birch returned to business. "I'm taking him back to Carson City."

Marshal Higgins squinted. "What's he supposed to have done?"

"Supposed to have murdered a rancher," Birch explained. "I need a place to hold him for the night."

The lawman got up and crossed the tiny room to pour himself another shot. He returned to his table.

Birch pointed out, "You forgot to leave your money on the counter."

"Ol' Sam and me have an agreement. When he's gone, I watch the place. In return, I get all the free liquor I can drink."

Birch raised his eyebrows. "Then why—"

"—did I insist on you paying for my drink?" Higgins raised his full glass to Clem Johnston and grinned. "It's just good business, stranger. Just good business. Say, what's your name, now that we've had a drink together?"

"Jefferson Birch."

The lawman turned to Birch's prisoner and asked gently, "And your name, son?"

Johnston looked sullenly from Birch to the marshal. "What does it matter?"

"Matters to me," Higgins replied. "Just because a man's been accused of a crime don't mean he ain't got a name."

Johnston appeared to warm up to the crusty old lawman. He told him his name.

The marshal had a holding cell in the back of the general store. The store owner was a burly man who looked more like a trapper than a merchant. He lived above the store. Birch was confident that the fellow could handle himself if Johnston tried to escape.

The cell was a small storage room with stacks of boxes. A narrow cot, a bucket of water and a battered basin to wash up in, and a chamber pot, were jammed into one corner, and there was a window with bars so the prisoner wouldn't be left completely in the dark during daylight hours. The room was also equipped with a metal mesh door that was short by about two inches from the floor, which could be padlocked from the outside. Clem Johnston was escorted into the room and Birch given the key.

Holding up the key, Birch asked, "What if you need it?"

The marshal made a face. "Unless the whole Dalton gang shows up, I don't think we'll lock up anyone tonight. Ain't got nothin' worth stealing. It ain't Saturday night, so it's not likely a citizen's gonna get drunk and tear up the town. I think young Johnston here's gonna have the whole place to hisself."

Birch and Higgins started to leave, but the marshal paused at the door and said in a kind voice to Johnston, "Oh, and you won't be starvin' none either, son. Mrs. Higgins is makin' her special fried chicken for dinner tonight and also bakes the best gooseberry pie this side of the Humboldt River. She'll be by soon and will slide it under that door there for you."

Birch thought he saw Clem Johnston perk up a bit before following the marshal out of the door. He wasn't sure why he liked this kid so much. Although Johnston had remained silent for the better part of their journey here, he didn't have that cold-blooded look that Birch had seen in so many killers.

Birch asked about the hotel.

Higgins shrugged. "Nothing fancy, but you can get a good night's rest there for an honest price. And you'll get a decent meal."

Birch ventured, "Is there anyone staying at the hotel right now?"

Marshal Higgins scratched his whiskered jaw. "Well now, I seem to recall this stall-fed tenderfoot gettin' off the stagecoach yesterday. Don't know if he traveled on or stayed."

The tenderfoot was probably his employer, Arthur Tisdale, and Birch wondered how long Tisdale would stay. He asked Marshal Higgins, "How often does the stagecoach come through here?"

"Oh, about twice a week. It won't be back for another few days. You planning on staying here until then?"

Birch frowned. He wanted to get Clem Johnston back to Carson City sooner than that. Besides, stagecoaches were notoriously slow and dangerous to ride in. Also, in the back of his mind, Birch didn't like the idea of riding in the same enclosed space with his employer for what could prove to be several days. It would be much better to travel by horse.

Besides, he didn't want to leave Cactus boarded here for a prolonged length of time.

"I think we'll be moving on tomorrow," Birch finally answered. "We can make just as good time traveling by horse if we start then. We should be in Carson City in a few days."

Marshal Higgins didn't look all that convinced. "Sounds pretty dangerous to me. There aren't too many towns between here and Virginia City, so you might get caught camping out a few nights with that prisoner."

Birch shrugged. "I don't think that will be a problem."

The lawman left Birch outside the hotel. "Well, if I don't see you tomorrow morning, good luck. The general store gets locked up at night, but you can get in tomorrow morning. Mrs. Higgins will bring breakfast over to the boy. After he finishes eating, just come on back and take him out, then leave the key in the padlock." Marshal Higgins paused, then added, "Birch, I know it ain't any of my business but that boy don't seem like a killer to me."

Birch extended his hand and said, "Marshal, thanks for your help."

CHAPTER 3

IN the early evening Arthur Tisdale took his daily constitutional around the town of Paradise Valley. It had been a habit since his days as an army officer. An hour's walk always piqued his appetite.

He had resigned from his duties almost three years ago. At first he'd traveled, but he soon tired of that. He had always been fascinated with law enforcement, but couldn't see pinning a badge on his chest. He didn't have enough education to become a lawyer, but with his administrative experience in the military, it seemed only reasonable that he form a private investigations agency.

Jefferson Birch, an ex–Texas Ranger, was the first experienced man to be hired, but that soon changed. Tisdale had since expanded and hired on more agents whenever he got assignments for them. It was not steady work: they took other jobs between assignments and Tisdale would wire an agent whenever he needed someone. But every one of them, with the exception of Birch, had drifted on, and Tisdale found it a frustrating experience to constantly be in the process of interviewing prospective agents.

That was why he had decided to accompany Birch on this assignment. He hoped to spend more time with his first agent and discover what qualities Birch had that made him stick with Tisdale Investigations. Maybe Tisdale could go back to his agency in San Francisco with a more substantial idea of what he was looking for when interviewing prospects.

That evening, Tisdale met up with Jefferson Birch in the hotel dining room. The ex–Texas Ranger looked clean and rested.

Birch nodded to Tisdale and they shook hands.

"I'm surprised you made it here so quickly, Mr. Tisdale," Birch said. "I'd expected to wait another day or two for your arrival."

"There were no delays for the stagecoach and no detours to other small out-of-the-way towns. It took only three days. I was certainly very lucky," Tisdale acknowledged. He stroked his mustache thoughtfully and asked, "So I presume you are here with the prisoner?"

Birch raised his eyebrows and replied, "Well, yes, I am. But what I don't understand is why you wanted to meet me out here. You could have waited in Carson City. There was no guarantee that I'd pick up Johnston's trail so quickly and capture him."

Tisdale chuckled. "I must have more faith in your tracking abilities than you do. Your record as a Ranger was exemplary and I was counting on your experience and loyalty."

Birch looked puzzled. Tisdale continued, "What I mean to say is that I knew you'd catch Clem Johnston. And I hate to admit this"—Tisdale took a deep breath—"but I'm a little naive when it comes to the sort of business we're in. Don't misunderstand me, Birch—I know all there is to know about running the business end of the agency. But I need to know more about the actual investigation and field work."

He caught Birch suppressing a smile. Tisdale pursed his lips in annoyance and said, "That's why I met you here. I want to watch you at work. I've had some trouble keeping agents, and I want to know what makes you tick. I need more men like you. So I'm accompanying you and your prisoner to Carson City."

A short silence followed. Finally, Birch cleared his throat. "You don't even have a horse," he pointed out. "And why this particular assignment? Why didn't you wait for a real investigation?"

Tisdale explained, "I want to see how you handle yourself with a prisoner and I thought there would be less interference on this assignment than if I were to visit during an in-depth investigation."

"Excuse me for asking this, Mr. Tisdale, but why do you need to be here at all? Maybe if we just sat down and talked for a few hours, you'd get the sort of information you need."

Tisdale nodded. It was a fair suggestion. "To be honest with you, Birch, I've been very impressed with the way you handle assignments. I know you've had to take other positions in between, but I expect that to change. When I first started this agency and hired you, I didn't know what I was looking for in an investigator, and it was sheer luck that you responded to my ad in the newspaper."

Birch's face remained impassive. He finally shook his head and said, "I don't know if I'll be much help to you. Sometimes I don't know myself why I leave a good job on a ranch to take on a case for you."

Tisdale smiled smugly. "You have a calling for this sort of work. You take chances, and once you get hold of a case, you won't let anything distract you from your duties. I was told by your former captain of your devotion to duty, even under some unexpected and tragic circumstances."

The former Ranger's expression clouded over and he remained silent.

In their first meeting, Tisdale had gotten a glimpse of Jefferson Birch's past, a past that held some unpleasant memories. He didn't press the issue at the time because Birch appeared to be a man of few words, and Arthur Tisdale respected that. Now he amended his last statement. "What I meant was that you have an ideal background for this type of work, Birch. I hope you don't think too seriously about leaving me in the lurch."

Birch's face relaxed some and he nodded gruffly. "I'll think about what you said, Mr. Tisdale. But there should be plenty of men with my type of background."

"My agency is on the verge," Tisdale continued enthusiastically, "of becoming known throughout the West." He leaned back, stuck his thumbs in his brocade vest pockets, and sighed contentedly.

"Have you ever traveled by horse for long distances before?" Birch asked warily.

Two platters of venison and mashed potatoes with gravy were put in front of them. Tisdale eyed his dinner hungrily, but Birch, apparently lost in thought, stared at his food without eating.

Tisdale smiled. "I probably haven't mentioned it before, but I was in the army for twenty years. I joined up when I turned seventeen."

"What rank?"

"Colonel when I left. Three years ago," Tisdale said between mouthfuls of food. "I rode a lot of horses. I know it's been a few years, but I think I could get back in the saddle again. I'll probably be slightly sore for the first day or two. But once a horseman, always a horseman, I always say."

Birch looked dubious, but said, "I guess we'll have to get you outfitted tomorrow."

"How long did it take you to catch Johnston?"

"A few days. I started following the trail the day after I got your wire."

Tisdale leaned forward, his elbows on the table. "Did you get a confession out of him?"

Birch appeared briefly uncomfortable. Then he stared down at his untouched dinner and said, "It was hard to get a word out of him." He shook his head. "I know he's wanted for murder, but what do you know about it?"

Tisdale had finished his meal and was contentedly stroking his mustache again. He waited for his plate to be cleared and his coffee mug to be refilled. A woman came out from the kitchen and placed a huge slab of hot gingerbread in front of him.

While waiting for his dessert to cool, Tisdale told Birch all he knew about the case. Clem Johnston had worked as a ranch hand for a man named Frank Ashton. He'd been on the job for a little under six months, and it was well known that they didn't get along. Several people had witnessed frequent arguments between Johnston and Ashton.

On the morning in question, Mrs. Ashton and her son John asked Clem Johnston to go out to the stable to hitch a horse to their buggy. They were going into Carson City to run a few errands. Frank Ashton had already gone out.

Johnston agreed and headed toward the barn. Ashton's son John later swore that a few minutes after Johnston left, he heard a loud argument in the stable. But at the time, John thought nothing of it. His father often raised his voice to the ranch hands when he was upset about something. When the horse and buggy weren't ready ten minutes later, John decided to go out and see if Johnston needed a hand.

The son was joined by his mother on the way to the barn. When they got to the door, they both saw Clem Johnston standing over the body of Frank Ashton, clutching a bloody knife in one hand.

Birch was silent during the account, but when Tisdale was finished, he asked, "Who hired Tisdale Investigations to bring Clem Johnston back?"

Tisdale answered, "The Ashtons. The law has put up a small reward, but we have the added incentive of being retained by Mrs. Ashton and her son. John Ashton is particularly anxious to find Clem Johnston and bring him back for trial. I didn't think it would be too difficult to find Clem Johnston. His kind are usually easily caught."

"His kind?" Birch asked with a curious expression on his face.

Leaning forward, Tisdale said, "Amateurs, people who aren't killers by nature. It seems that Frank Ashton was no angel. Plenty of people hated him. I think it happened this way—Johnston and Ashton fought, Ashton threatened his ranch hand. In a heated moment, Johnston pulled a knife and stabbed his employer." Tisdale leaned back in his chair. "It's as simple as that."

Birch raised his eyebrows. "Well, I guess that's what the trial will determine, right?"

"Right," Tisdale said with satisfaction. "We're to deliver him to the sheriff in Carson City and travel out to the Ashton place to collect our fee."

Tisdale paid for their meal, and they left the hotel to stroll down the street to the saloon. Tisdale cleared his throat and said, "So tomorrow we can pick out a horse and some traveling gear for me. It's been a long time . . ."

They turned into the saloon and went to the bar. Tisdale looked around for the bartender, but the small rudimentary saloon was empty. Coins and gold nuggets lay on the counter and several empty bottles and used glasses were clustered together at one end. He looked at Birch questioningly.

Looking mildly amused, Birch explained, "The bartender is out of town getting supplies. The marshal told me to help myself here and leave the money on the counter."

It was Tisdale's turn to raise his eyebrows. "What trust these people must have in each other." He watched Birch move behind the counter, pick out a dusty bottle of brandy, and pour two healthy glasses.

"As I was saying," Tisdale continued, "I'm afraid it's been some time since I've ridden a horse." He looked up and noticed that Birch left his brandy untouched. Instead, he was pouring a third glass. Tisdale frowned. "What are you doing?"

Birch picked up both drinks and replied, "I'm going to check on our prisoner. After that, I'm going to turn in. It's been a long day for me. See you at breakfast." With that, he nodded and left.

Tisdale drained his glass and looked around at the empty room. *I was hoping to trade war stories with him,* he thought.

He briefly wondered if he should have gone with his agent to visit Clem Johnston. After a moment, Tisdale shrugged. There would be time for that. It was enough for Tisdale to know that Birch was conscientious enough to check on the prisoner. He poured himself a second glass of the brandy.

CHAPTER 4

IT was quiet in the general store. Clem Johnston was sitting in his cell, finishing up a piece of gooseberry pie. Birch placed the two glasses of brandy on top of a crate and lit an aging kerosene lamp that was perched on the edge of a table. Johnston looked up, the morose expression on his face accentuated by the deepening shadows.

"What do you want?" he asked in a sullen tone.

Birch raised one of the glasses. "I thought you might want a drink to wash that down with." He pushed it under the cage door.

Johnston picked it up and sniffed it. "What is this stuff? It don't smell like red-eye."

Birch sipped his brandy silently, inwardly amused at the kid's bravado. He had seen earlier that Johnston couldn't hold his liquor any better than a leaky bucket could hold water.

Johnston tasted it and, in a grudging tone, admitted, "Not bad." Looking expectantly at his captor, he asked, "Why are you still here?"

"Thought you could use some company. It's bad enough being locked up in a real jail cell with lawmen coming and going, but being cooped up in this empty store . . ."

Birch looked around at the crates that filled the storeroom. With only the forlorn lamp flame flickering in the darkness, he couldn't put himself in Johnston's place. The prisoner couldn't even keep a lit candle in his cell because he might cause a fire. It was a gloomy place at night.

Johnston eyed Birch with suspicion. "You want to hear my side of the story, I suppose."

Birch replied easily, "If you want to tell it."

"What if I told you I was innocent? What would you do then, let me out?" Johnston put his drink down and, his hands clinging to the mesh, pressed himself against the metal cage door like a desperate animal. He leveled his gaze at Birch and said with a sneer, "Or did you really come down here to get me drunk and maybe get a confession out of me?"

Birch drained his brandy and chuckled. "On one brandy?" He pointed a finger at the young prisoner and added, "You don't trust anyone, do you? Is that what got you into this mess in the first place?"

"Get the hell out and leave me alone!" Johnston turned away and dropped back onto his cot.

Birch shook his head at the young man and started to back out. He paused in the doorway and called out, "Maybe you'll feel more like talking tomorrow, kid. You know, I came here tonight to hear what you had to say. No judgments. I just like to make sure I'm taking the right man in."

"I'll gladly tell you I'm not Clem Johnston, if that's what you want to hear."

"I want to hear your version of Ashton's murder," said Birch.

He waited for a reply, but Johnston remained silent. Birch extinguished the lamp before leaving.

Outside, heading for the hotel, Birch thought he'd give it another try tomorrow when they were on the road. There was something about this case that just didn't feel right. He'd had this feeling many times before, and nine times out of ten it panned out.

Maybe it was just that when cornered on that cliff, Clem Johnston had been reluctant to kill him to save his own neck. Birch hoped that while they were traveling, Johnston would become more talkative.

Birch remembered, with a sinking feeling, that Arthur Tisdale would be along. He wasn't looking forward to being hampered by a man who hadn't ridden a horse for three years. And he had a suspicion that Tisdale's being there would make it more difficult for Johnston to talk openly about the Ashton killing. Furthermore, if Birch did discover that this case wasn't what it appeared to be, Tisdale was unlikely to let him investigate without a paying client.

Birch reached the entrance to the hotel. It had just turned dark, and suddenly he was very weary.

The next morning, Birch met Tisdale in the hotel dining room. Dark puffy circles under Tisdale's eyes made it abundantly clear to Birch that his employer must have drunk the entire bottle of brandy the night before.

Birch greeted him anyway. "Good mor—"

Tisdale held up a hand to stop him. They sat down.

"I don't think I can eat much this morning," Tisdale whispered. "Just coffee."

Birch was amused and decided to take advantage of his employer's condition. "No, Mr. Tisdale. We'll be on the road until dark, and I don't think riding on an empty stomach is such a good idea."

Tisdale looked miserable, but he didn't seem to have the heart to argue. Birch ordered two big breakfasts. They ate in silence.

After breakfast, Birch accompanied his employer to the stable and, after haggling with the swarthy owner for a fair price, bought a horse and saddle. A pair of denims, two cotton shirts, and a bedroll at the general store completed Tisdale's outfitting.

While Tisdale got ready, Birch led Cactus and Johnston's nag, Sweet Betsy, back over to the general store, handcuffed Clem Johnston, and sat him on his horse. It was midmorning when they met Tisdale at the edge of town and began the ride south. Birch's employer appeared to have sufficiently recovered from his binge the night before.

Birch told Clem Johnston, "This is my employer, Arthur Tisdale of Tisdale Investigations."

Johnston stared at Tisdale. "You're here to see a wanted man captured and returned for justice, huh?"

Arthur Tisdale's eyes widened, and he stroked his large mustache with a thoughtful look on his face. "I suppose you could look at it like that."

"Neither of you have any interest in seeing real justice done then, do you?" Clem Johnston's bound hands clenched and unclenched and a vein popped out in his neck, throbbing with anger. "Maybe you'll stay in Carson City for my hanging."

Tisdale blinked at Johnston's quiet rage. He replied, "What do you mean?"

Johnston looked away in a visible effort to contain his anger. Shrugging, he explained in a level voice, "I mean that this is business for you. It's just a way to make money. You're not interested in investigating Frank Ashton's death to find the real killer, are you?"

Birch had been quietly listening to this exchange. It was time to interrupt. Before Tisdale could reply, Birch answered Johnston, "I said it last night and I'll say it again, Johnston. If you want to tell me your version, I'm interested. I don't believe a man's guilty until I hear his side of the story as well."

Tisdale started to protest, but Birch shot him a look and he fell silent.

Clem Johnston turned away from both Birch and Tisdale, his eyes gazing straight ahead, and he began softly, "It was early in the morning. I'd just come out of the bunkhouse—it was my turn to make breakfast for the other ranch hands—and I met Mrs. Ashton. She asked me to get the buggy ready. She and her son John were going into town later. Of course, I agreed.

"Before I left, I asked where Mr. Ashton had gone off to.

She'd seen him go off early that morning to search for some missing cattle."

Clem Johnston shifted in his saddle and continued recounting the Ashton murder. "I was relieved to hear that he was gone for the day. Everyone knew we'd had a big fight the week before. He'd deducted the cost of a new saddle from my pay because the old one I'd been using had fallen apart. He told me it was my fault, that I hadn't taken care of the old saddle, but it was just that he was trying to get something for nothing, like always. Always trying to cheat an honest man out of his pay."

Birch interrupted. "Was this the first time he'd lowered a ranch hand's pay?"

"I wasn't the only ranch hand he'd done that to. Just about everyone who worked for him had their reasons for hating the man." Johnston laughed humorlessly. "But I was the only one who ever stood up to him. Look what it got me."

Birch stared thoughtfully ahead at the horizon and said, "It doesn't sound like an argument over an old saddle would be reason enough for you to kill him."

Johnston nodded in agreement. "I could have just packed up and moved on to another ranch. And in fact, I was thinking about it as I walked toward the barn to get Mrs. Ashton's buggy ready. That was when I heard them arguing."

Birch asked, "Who were arguing?"

Johnston paused for a moment and considered. "I recognized Mr. Ashton's voice. The other voice sounded familiar in a way, but it was a high voice . . ." Johnston stopped to think, then shook his head and said, "I just can't place it. I've been trying to ever since that day." He sighed and continued, "Anyway, I couldn't hear what they were fighting about. I didn't think much of it because Frank Ashton argued with everyone, but I didn't want to interrupt them and have Mr. Ashton mad at me as well. So I stayed over by the corral until they stopped arguing. When it was quiet I figured they must be finished, so I went into the barn.

"It was dim in there after being out in the bright sun. I almost stumbled over the body. It was the first thing I saw when my eyes adjusted." Clem Johnston's face paled at his next words. "And the knife was lying beside the body. He'd been stabbed and was all bloody."

"Why did you pick up the knife?"

Clem Johnston looked at Birch as if he were surprised he'd asked that question. "I'd seen the knife before. I recognized the hilt and the unusual curved blade."

Tisdale frowned. "Why didn't you tell the marshal that when he came to get you?"

Johnston slumped in his saddle again. "I don't remember where I saw it or who it belonged to. I just knew I'd seen it before."

Something suddenly occurred to Birch and he asked, "Before you went into the barn, did you see anyone leave?"

Clem Johnston hung his head and his hair covered his face. "No. I've been over it and over it in my head and I don't remember seeing anyone coming out of the barn. Of course, it would've been easy for someone to sneak out the back door of the barn or climb up in the hayloft and shinny down the rope that hangs from one of the doors."

Birch added, "Or hide in the barn while you came in."

Johnston looked up. "So you believe me?"

"Did you hear anyone up in the loft?"

Johnston shook his head. "But he could have gone out the back, like I mentioned before."

Birch nodded encouragement. "So you walked into the barn and almost tripped over Frank Ashton's body. You looked down, recognized the knife, and picked it up."

Johnston picked it up from there. "That was when Mrs. Ashton and her son John came in. I didn't have any time to explain. John drew his gun and called to a nearby ranch hand to go get the marshal."

Birch frowned. "No one asked you what happened?"

Johnston looked grim. "I didn't stick around to see . . ."

Tisdale said, "You should have waited until the marshal came, then told him your story."

Both Birch and Johnston turned to stare at him.

"That's what you'd have done?" Johnston asked Tisdale. "And what if they didn't listen, found you guilty, and threw a little necktie party right then and there?"

Tisdale puffed his chest out and said, "That would never happen. They would listen to me because—"

"—you were innocent?" Birch asked simply.

Tisdale peered at his agent sharply, but said nothing. Clem Johnston looked on silently, the ghost of a smile on his thin, handsome face.

Birch turned back to the accused killer and asked, "Is there anyone you suspect? Someone who might have had a motive for killing Frank Ashton? Was Ashton disliked by other ranch owners?"

Johnston gave a short nod. "Everyone hated him. Most of the ranch owners in the valley, quite a few merchants in Carson City, saloon owners, even his wife and son."

"His wife and son?" Birch asked.

"Frank Ashton was a hard man. There was talk that he beat his wife. No one ever saw it happen, but she had an awful lot of 'accidents.' And everyone knew he had other women when he was out on cattle drives. He never made it a secret."

Even Tisdale was getting interested in what the accused man had to say. He asked, "And what about John, his son?"

"Now he's a strange one. But I don't blame John Ashton for that. He was a disappointment to his father, and John didn't much like working for him. Mr. Ashton treated him pretty bad."

They all fell silent, Birch's mind turning over the other possibilities.

He broke the silence to ask, "How did you escape?"

For the first time since Birch laid eyes on him, Clem Johnston looked genuinely amused. "John held a gun on me until the marshal got there. Then all hell broke loose. I think Mrs. Ashton started it, but I couldn't swear to it. It seemed to me that she bumped into John accidentally, which caused him to drop his gun. The marshal was just walking up to the barn. I got hold of John's gun and made the marshal and the other ranch hands toss their irons into a nearby haystack. Then I grabbed the nearest saddled horse and left."

Birch smiled. Tisdale's response was more cynical, a loud "Humph!" emerging from beneath his ridiculously large mustache.

There didn't seem to be much more to say, so the three men rode on in silence. Birch turned his attention to the landscape. Mountains lay to both sides, covered with small juniper trees that grew up the vast, sweeping sides of the ranges. They reached the Humboldt River by midafternoon and continued to follow it downstream. Soon the land gave way to sandy hillocks and no shade. Birch squinted to his right and saw a vast expanse of desert.

Johnston was watching him with interest. "You haven't been this way before, have you?"

Taking his hat off and wiping his forehead with a sleeve, Birch said, "No. I picked up your trail from Willow, where I was working on a ranch. Then, as you know, I followed you out of Pine Ridge. I haven't had a chance to explore this area much since I got here."

Tisdale piped up, "You should be used to desert where you come from, Birch."

The ex–Texas Ranger noticed that Tisdale had dispensed with the formality of addressing him as "Mr. Birch." He replied, "I'm used to hot weather and arid land, that's for sure. I'm not sure I'd call Texas a desert, though."

Tisdale and Johnston looked at each other. Birch assumed that neither of them had ever been to Texas. How could he describe it to them? It was more to him than just low mountain ranges, high plateaus, and springs; it was Audrey and their ranch house built with his own hands; it was his job with the Rangers that took him away from his very pregnant wife. It was supposed to be a simple job, according to the Ranger captain who promised that Birch would be back in time for the birth of his child.

The assignment took him down to the Rio Grande, where he was to wait for a fugitive horse thief to be brought back across the border by the Mexican army. It took longer than either the captain or Birch had thought. When he returned to his home, his wife and baby had been laid to rest. To this day, Birch couldn't help but feel that if he'd been there, he might have prevented Audrey from dying. Maybe even prevented his son from dying, too.

He didn't try to explain any of this to Tisdale and Johnston. Instead, Birch shrugged and replied, "Maybe you're right. I'm used to the desert." He looked at the sun, which was starting to sink in the western sky. "We'd better start looking for a campsite after crossing these sand hills."

CHAPTER 5

THE land didn't get much better as they rode on into the afternoon. Birch continued to lead his prisoner and Tisdale along the Humboldt. Scatterings of grass dotted the riverbank, and the tangy scent of sagebrush rode with them. Once the desert valley gave way to a new mountain range to their right, the scrubby sagebrush, bitter brush, and mesquite spread out as far as Birch's eye could see.

Birch noticed that Tisdale had been looking uncomfortable in his saddle for the last ten miles. When they reached a low grassy butte, he decided it was time to set up camp. A few trees provided shelter and Birch secured his prisoner to the twisted limb of a juniper.

He'd just gone over to check on Cactus and get food for their evening meal and his bedroll when Tisdale sidled over and said in a low voice, "You don't really believe that poppycock the boy was telling you, do you?"

Birch paused, then said very deliberately, "Look, Mr. Tisdale. You may be my boss when it comes to doling out pay, and you have a right to expect a job done well. But that doesn't mean I have to like the job I do. Or believe in it."

Tisdale pulled back, obviously offended by Birch's tone. "I didn't mean it that way."

Birch softened his tone and asked, "How did you mean it?"

Tisdale paused before replying. "I just don't believe him, and I think you're intelligent enough to know a shady story when you hear one. I heard plenty during my time as a colonel. And I don't think I need remind you that our client isn't paying us to look into this murder."

Birch sighed. It was time to change the subject. "We need some wood for a fire. Think you can handle that, sir?"

Birch felt that despite Tisdale's having been in the army, the man was almost useless. This was confirmed when Tisdale came back empty-handed, explaining that he'd searched the area for wood and found none. Birch shook his head and went in search of twigs and branches to make a fire.

When he got back to camp with an armful, there was a chill in the air. Tisdale was in the process of scooping coffee grounds into the battered coffee pot that Birch had tied to the side of his saddle. A slab of bacon was ready to be fried up in a small flat cast-iron pan, and grits were soaking in water in the accompanying cast-iron saucepan.

Feeling slightly relieved that Tisdale wasn't proving to be totally helpless, Birch dug a pit in the sandy soil and piled his wood in it. Taking one of the oily rags he kept handy in one of his saddle pouches, he stuffed it under the pyramid of wood and took a flint out of his pocket to light it. After giving off a thick black smoke that everyone avoided breathing in, the wood caught fire and they began cooking their dinner.

It wasn't as fine a meal as at the Paradise Valley Hotel the night before, but Birch enjoyed the sunset, the cool breeze that accompanied the twilight, and the hush that fell over the countryside at this time every day. Even Johnston and Tisdale seemed to be enjoying it, because they hadn't said a word since camp was set up.

Birch was just drifting off to sleep near the fire when the sound of a woman sobbing woke him up with a start. Tisdale was already up, at the edge of the campsite. The fire was burning low and Birch automatically stoked it. He glanced over at the prisoner, who was also watching Tisdale attentively.

Birch drew his gun as a precaution. A moment later, Tisdale came back into the light of the campfire, a young bedraggled woman leaning on his left shoulder.

Her face was streaked with dirt and the left shoulder of her plain brown dress was torn, as was a portion of the bodice and the hem. Her chestnut hair had at one time been pinned up, but was now half undone and tangled. She was shaking.

"Don't just stand there, Birch," Tisdale ordered in clipped military fashion. "Get this young lady some water."

Birch eyed the darkness from where she'd staggered into camp before reluctantly holstering his gun. From a canteen, he poured some water into a tin mug and handed it to the distressed stranger, feeling slightly uneasy about the situation.

She took the cup gratefully, cupping her hands around it, and drinking deeply from it.

Tisdale sat close to her, his eyes filled with concern. His demeanor suggested that he would take charge of this distraught woman. Birch was quietly amused.

A glance over at Johnston told Birch that the captive was taking this whole scene with a great deal of calm. In fact, Johnston's eyes were closed in feigned sleep. Birch didn't like it one bit; there was something strange going on here. But the only thing Birch had to go on was a feeling.

Finishing her coffee, the woman closed her eyes briefly, then opened them and looked at the three men as if for the first time. She started and visibly shuddered.

Tisdale said in a fatherly tone, "Now please don't be frightened, madam. We're here to help you. If you feel up to it, please tell us your name and what happened."

She appeared to calm down a bit and began her story. "My name is Emma. My husband and I were traveling south to Virginia City. We were just crossing the desert valley back there when we were attacked by a band of outlaws."

Birch leaned forward and asked, "Where is your husband?"

Emma sobbed. "He was trying to defend me when those outlaws killed him. I managed to escape." She wiped her tears away with the ragged hem of her skirt. "We were going to start a new life in Virginia City. Tom had a good job waiting for him. I'd give anything to have Tom back with me." She collapsed, her face hidden by the folds of her skirt. Tisdale patted her shoulder.

Birch shifted uncomfortably, settling his back against his saddle. For some reason he couldn't explain, he didn't feel her pain. Maybe he was too busy being suspicious of everyone whose path they would cross on the journey to Carson City. Maybe Birch was hardened by his own pain.

Birch cleared his throat and said, "Well, I suppose we could all backtrack into the desert tomorrow and find your husband."

"For a decent burial," Tisdale added.

For a moment, Emma looked startled. Then she relaxed and gave them a sad smile. "I . . . I don't think I could go back there," Emma said softly, wrapping her arms around her in emphasis. "What if they're still there?"

"Don't worry, you're safe with us." Tisdale turned to Birch and said, "Maybe we should move on tonight."

Clem Johnston piped up from the edge of the campfire, "I won't mind, of course. We could all go dig this woman's husband a proper grave. Seems to be the fitting thing to do."

Birch glared first at Tisdale, then Johnston. Finally, he turned to Emma and said, "In your grief, you may not have noticed that we're escorting a prisoner back to Carson City. You can stay with us tonight and move on with us tomorrow, but I think it would be best if we leave you at the first way station or town we come to." Turning to Tisdale, he added firmly, "And tonight, I think it'll be best if we take turns on watch."

Tisdale protested. "Now wait a minute, Birch. I'm your superior and I think . . ."

Emma interrupted. "Thank you, gentlemen, for your kind offers." She gave warm looks to both Tisdale and Johnston, then continued, "But I think this man's plan is just fine. I don't want to be a burden and certainly don't want to upset your plans. If you will just let me curl up by the fire . . ."

Tisdale jumped up and touched her arm. "Madam, I wouldn't dream of letting you sleep on the cold, hard ground. I insist that you take my bedroll."

She had opened her mouth to protest when, smiling wryly, Birch said, "You might as well take him up on his offer, ma'am. Only one of us will be asleep at a time tonight. Whoever is not on guard can use my bedroll."

Emma thanked them both graciously and crawled into Tisdale's blankets.

Tisdale looked on until he appeared to be satisfied that she was comfortable. Then he approached Birch, who was still propped up against his saddle, halfway out of his bedroll. He looked expectantly at his agent.

Birch raised an eyebrow. "What?" With a curt nod, he said, "Oh, yes. You'll be needing this tonight."

With that, he drew his gun, checked the bullet chamber, and handed it to a surprised Tisdale. His boss handled it in such a clumsy manner that Birch winced inwardly.

Crossing his arms and trying to keep the sarcasm out of his voice, Birch asked, "You know how to use a gun, don't you?"

Tisdale replied, "Of course I do. Learned it in the army."

Tisdale stood there a moment more, then moved off just beyond the waning glow of the campfire. Birch called after him, "Wake me up in about four hours. I'll take the second watch."

Birch smiled to himself. He hoped Tisdale was a fair shot with a gun. He also hoped Tisdale wouldn't start shooting at shadows, because if those outlaws were real, Birch didn't want Tisdale to do anything to attract their attention.

There was something about the woman that bothered him, but after hearing her story, he supposed that it could have happened. Besides, she had sided with him about being left at the nearest sign of civilization.

Of course, there was the fact that Tisdale was now on guard duty until the wee hours of the morning. An ex-Army colonel doing sentry duty—that was enough to worry even the most trusting soul. Putting his head back on his well-worn saddle and closing his eyes, Birch knew that he wouldn't get much sleep during the next four hours.

CHAPTER 6

BIRCH had closed his eyes for what felt like only a matter of minutes. Suddenly Tisdale was standing over him, shaking his shoulder. Rubbing the grit from his eyes, the ex-Ranger struggled out of his blankets as quietly as possible. Tisdale handed him the Navy Colt and switched places with Birch.

Tisdale slipped into the bedroll with only a short comment, "It's all quiet out there," before curling up against the saddle and closing his eyes.

Taking deep breaths to shake the sleep from his body, Birch noticed a slight movement by the campfire. With his hand on his gun, he moved closer before realizing that Emma was heating up a pot of coffee over the dying embers.

Birch approached her and asked in a low voice, "What are you doing up at this hour? You should be getting some sleep."

Emma looked up at him and smiled. It was a pretty smile. She'd cleaned her face up and untangled her hair, tying it back with a strip of cloth that looked like it might have once belonged to a petticoat.

"I can't sleep," she replied. "And I thought I'd be of more use making coffee for your vigil than lying in the bedroll feeling sorry for myself."

"I'm sorry about your husband," Birch said with more than a little empathy. "I wish I could say that as time goes on, the memory will dim and you'll feel better."

"Thank you," Emma said, adding in a rueful voice, "I appreciate your honesty. I have a feeling that I'll hear plenty of platitudes when I reach Virginia City."

Birch was starting to feel a little guilty. Why shouldn't he

34

believe her? The pain in her voice was evident and her loss was more immediate than his. Sometimes Birch wondered if he'd ever get over grieving for his wife. And sometimes he wondered if his continued grieving was not so much for the loss of his loved ones as for the loss of his way of life.

She handed him a steaming tin cup of coffee. Their eyes met. There was an uncomfortable silence.

Birch backed away slightly, breaking the spell. Emma must have felt the same way because she lowered her eyes and self-consciously slid her hands slowly down the front of her skirt.

Birch took a sip of his coffee and said, "Well, thank you for the trouble you've gone to. You'd better get some sleep. I'll be waking everyone early so we can get started."

Avoiding his eyes, Emma nodded and replied, "You're welcome." As she headed back to her bedroll, Emma paused and added, "And thank you. For taking me in." With that, she crawled under a blanket and appeared to go to sleep.

Birch walked around the camp and checked on everyone. Even in his uncomfortable position, Clem Johnston appeared to be asleep. There was no question that Tisdale was asleep—his snoring could be heard across the campsite.

Birch drained his coffee and walked to the edge of the camp. He was feeling slightly woozy, probably from being awakened after only a few hours of sleep. *The cool air will wake me up*, he thought.

He patroled the border of the camp, acutely aware of even the smallest sound. After a complete stroll around the camp, there was little for Birch to do except crouch by a juniper tree.

His eyes still felt grainy and he wished there were a stream nearby to splash water on his face. Although they were following the Humboldt, the rough trail sometimes followed the river closely and at other times meandered away. The camp was just a little over a mile away from the river.

Birch blinked several times in rapid succession, hoping for the feeling to go away. He'd accepted the coffee because, unlike the common theory that coffee relaxes a person, he'd found that it helped to keep him awake, although it wasn't working too well now. He was starting to feel drowsy, and his eyelids felt like lead. Birch stood and stretched in an effort to wake up his muscles.

Trying to suppress a yawn, he finally gave in to his weariness and closed his eyes. It'll only be for a moment, Birch thought as he yawned again. I'll get up in five minutes and patrol the area again.

The sensation of growing warmth spread over Birch's face. When he tried to open his eyes, he squinted against the glare, then lifted a hand to shield his eyes from the sun. He tried to remember where he was.

Birch remembered setting up camp last night and a woman named Emma staggering in with a tale of murderous outlaws and a dead husband. Everything after that was fuzzy.

Birch sat up, too quickly. His head ached the way it did when he'd had too much to drink the night before, but there wasn't a saloon within twenty miles of where he sat. His hand knocked over a tin cup, coffee dregs spilling out on the hard ground. The possibility that Emma had slipped something into his coffee slowly dawned on him.

When he finally looked around, he noticed that Tisdale's bedroll was gone, but his own bedroll was still there, blankets flung aside as if someone had left them in haste. Clem Johnston's handcuffs were left deserted underneath a tree. Birch tried to jump to his feet, tripped on a canteen lying nearby, and landed hard on his hip. His hand automatically went to his holster—but it was empty.

The campfire was cold. His horse, Cactus, was gone, as were the other two horses. Birch's saddle, which he'd used last night to rest his head on, had been taken, along with his saddlebags. His money and Bowie knife had been stashed in the bags, and his rifle had been in its own holster.

For a moment, Birch let the anger surge. He'd been taken

in by that woman. Emma must have been acquainted with Johnston. The accused killer could never have gotten loose on his own; even if he had, why would he have abducted the woman? And where was Tisdale?

Birch studied the immediate area, but found no sign of a struggle other than the unmade bedroll. All three horses were gone. Had Tisdale woken to find Clem Johnston and Emma sneaking out of camp? Or already gone? Did he then go after them? Or did they take him as a hostage?

Birch shook his head. If Tisdale had awakend to find the prisoner gone, he would surely have also woken his agent to go in pursuit. Tisdale must have been taken along, for whatever reason.

Birch couldn't think clearly until he got up to walk around and clear his head out. He was angry at himself for believing Emma's story. What now? He looked around the campsite in the vain hope that his gun had fallen on the ground or gotten lodged under a fallen log. After a quick but thorough search that yielded nothing, Birch gave up.

With an exasperated sigh, he slung the canteen around his shoulder and followed the horse tracks out of the campsite. They were headed south toward the Humboldt River. He knew that if he moved fast, he might catch up with them in the next town, if they stayed overnight. On foot, it was very difficult to cover lost ground when your quarry had all the horses.

Birch pulled his canteen up and checked the contents. At least there was some water left in it. He paused to splash cold water on his face, then walked on at a fairly fast pace. Maybe he had a chance of catching up to them, but so far, he didn't feel very lucky today.

CHAPTER 7

TISDALE groaned. He'd never been shot before. It hurt like hell. He was lucky it was a clean wound. The bullet had only grazed his shoulder, but he was having a devil of a time trying to stop the bleeding. He was starting to wonder why he'd thought he could go after Clem Johnston and Emma alone.

It hadn't occurred to Tisdale that although he was an army man, his experience didn't qualify him for running after outlaws. Especially since he didn't have a weapon. In fact, it was beyond his comprehension why he'd ever decided to accompany Jefferson Birch on a journey like this. It had appeared to be an easy undertaking on the face of it— obviously he had been wrong.

It was still before dawn, and the air had an autumn chill in it that made him shiver involuntarily. Tisdale winced as he peeled his shirt away from the injury. Privately, he had to admit that his pride was more damaged than his shoulder, for it was Emma who had discovered him following them. And it was she who had shot him.

It had happened earlier that morning: Tisdale had awoken to the whispers and scufflings of Johnston and Emma. At first it was hard for the retired Army colonel to believe that the seemingly helpless creature he'd sat beside earlier that night, whose shoulder he'd patted as she mourned the loss of a nonexistent husband, was now aiding the escape of a killer.

From his bedroll, feigning sleep, he spied Birch sprawled awkwardly against a juniper tree. Had Emma knocked Birch out or, worse, killed him? Again, it was hard for him to believe, but the evidence was too overwhelming. She must have been the one to put Birch out of commission because at that very moment, she was fiddling with the handcuffs, trying to free Clem Johnston. Finally, a loud metallic click, and Johnston was standing, rubbing his wrists.

Tisdale bided his time, catching part of their subdued discussion.

"Should we leave a horse for them?" Emma asked.

"Why should we?" Johnston muttered. "We might as well leave them all the horses and go on foot, if that's the case."

Emma expressed surprise. "But surely two men on one horse won't be able to catch up with us!"

In the dim gray light, Clem Johnston shook his head. "What makes you think that both men will use the horse? Maybe one man will leave the other behind while he tries to catch up with us."

Johnston got up, stretched his legs, started to pace, then turned to Emma and said in a fierce tone, "Even if they ride the one horse to the next town, what makes you think they won't buy another horse and set out after us again? Birch found me the first time—"

Emma interrupted. "I can't leave them without a horse," she whispered stubbornly. After a pause, she sounded more reasonable. "Besides, I doctored Birch's coffee. As for the other one, well . . ."

Johnston sighed. "He seems pretty harmless. I guess we'll take the chance."

With that, they quietly led two of the horses out of the campsite. When they were out of sight, Tisdale cautiously slipped out of his bedroll. Harmless! He'd never been so insulted in all his life.

Tisdale hesitated. What was he to do? There was no telling when Birch would wake, depending on what she used. Tisdale crawled over to his agent's prone form and shook Birch's arm, trying to wake him up.

"Birch! Birch!" Tisdale dared not shout his agent's name,

in case his voice would carry. He settled for a loud whisper. "Birch! Wake up! Johnston's escaping."

When it became clear that Jefferson Birch was in a deep sleep, Tisdale searched for Birch's gun. Which was gone.

Tisdale sat back on his heels. Of course it was gone, he reasoned. Would Johnston and his female accomplice leave a gun back here with men who, when they discovered Johnston had escaped, would most likely go after them? Tisdale was frustrated.

At least there was the horse. He glanced over, noticing that they had left Johnston's nag. Johnston and Emma had only been gone a few minutes. Was there a chance he could catch up, maybe ambush them? He did have the element of surprise in his favor. And he would relish the look on Johnston's face when he discovered that the man whom he'd dismissed as harmless had recaptured them.

And so he went after them, with determination.

You're a foolish old man, Tisdale now thought bitterly as he clumsily searched with his left hand for a handkerchief to stanch the blood. He sighed in exasperation, flinching at his memory of recent events.

He'd taken that nag, Sweet Betsy, and ridden after Johnston and Emma. The ground began to level out as they approached the river, heading south. Scrub brush became scarce and the sun was rising fast in the east. Tisdale was afraid he would be spotted. He would have to move in soon, but he had no weapon with him. It was then that Johnston and Emma dismounted their horses by the river.

It was now or never for Arthur Tisdale. He dismounted Sweet Betsy and gathered two large rocks. He led the nag to a large bitter brush and loosely tied the reins to it.

Stepping out from behind the bush, he heaved both rocks, one after the other, into the river. Johnston's and Emma's heads snapped in that direction. As an added distraction, he slapped Sweet Betsy's quarters, sending her careening out from behind the bitter brush while Tisdale ran full tilt toward Clem Johnston.

He caught the accused killer in the gut and they both went down, rolling on the muddy banks of the Humboldt. Amidst the scrambling, Tisdale managed to gain the upper hand, straddling Johnston's back and pinning his arms behind him. That was when he began searching for the gun. That was when he discovered that it was not Johnston, but Emma, who had the pistol.

He found himself staring full face down its barrel, the young woman supporting the gun with two very shaky hands.

"Get off of him," she ordered, her voice trembling.

Tisdale tried to reason with her. "Madam, Emma," he pleaded, "please give that to me. This man is extremely dangerous. I don't think you know what you're doing . . ."

A deafening explosion followed by something that felt like a forceful blow to his shoulder propelled him backward. He lay on the ground, stunned. How had he managed to end up in this position? The last thing he remembered was capturing Clem Johnston. He tried to get up, but found he couldn't move. Tisdale found it hard to breathe.

Sounds and voices floated above him. A high-pitched woman's scream, then a sob. "I've killed him!"

A calmer, more rational response from a man. "No, you haven't. I think you just knocked him out."

The woman replied, "Look, he's bleeding. Oh, I know I've killed him. I'm a real murderer, Clem!"

Clem Johnston sounded a little more impatient this time. "I don't think so, Em. Let me see."

Tisdale felt a hand on his chest and his shoulder, probing around the wound. He jumped when the hand touched his shoulder, but he felt too groggy to get up. His shoulder felt sore and tender, like it was filled with hot lead. Tisdale heard himself groan.

Johnston said, "No, he'll be fine. He just needs to clean the wound. The bullet grazed his shoulder. Come on. We have to go."

A pause, then, "Come on, Em. There's nothing we can do for him that he can't do for himself. Silly old fool."

The woman whimpered. The creak of leather, then the sound of horse's hoofs droning rhythmically away from the river.

With that, there was more quiet. After what seemed like an eternity, Tisdale attempted to move again and found it easier this time. He was sitting up, daubing at his bloody shoulder when Birch came into view.

Tisdale stopped, forgetting his pain momentarily at the sight of such a welcome face.

"Birch! Thank heavens you found me."

His agent looked annoyed for a moment, then concern took over as Birch took in Tisdale's disheveled appearance.

Birch kneeled beside him. "What happened to you?"

Tisdale shuddered involuntarily. "I woke up in the camp and heard them talking. The woman said she'd slipped a little something in your coffee."

Birch rubbed his head. "When that woman came into our camp, I should have trusted my instincts." He shook his head and looked around. "They took all the horses."

"And the gun, too," Tisdale said dryly.

Birch inspected the wound and washed it with a patch of cloth torn from Tisdale's shirttail. With another strip of shirt, he fashioned a sling so Tisdale wouldn't move his arm around too much until they reached the nearest town.

Birch stood up and scrutinized his handiwork. "There. That's about all I can do for you until we can get a doctor to look at it."

Tisdale managed a smile, which felt more like a grimace. "I feel just fine."

The ex–Texas Ranger grunted and adjusted his hat. "Yeah. My idea of feeling fine is a hot bath and a bottle. If you feel just fine after being shot at close range, you're a better man than me."

Tisdale chuckled. Birch helped him up, then looked around him, studying the ground.

Tisdale ventured a question. "Which way did they go?"

Taking his hat off, Birch scratched his head and replied, "Looks like they've gone south. They're following the Humboldt the same way we would have gone if Johnston hadn't escaped."

Tisdale shifted his wounded arm slightly into a more comfortable position. "This wouldn't have happened if I hadn't been along, would it? I mean, if I hadn't insisted on helping that girl."

Birch remained silent, studying the ground. Finally, he said, "Actually, no. What would have happened is that I probably would have taken the girl into camp despite my suspicions. The truth is, I couldn't have let her stay out there by herself any more than you could have. It takes me longer to trust a stranger when I'm working on a case, but I would have been taken in just the same—"

Tisdale interrupted. "You couldn't have known she'd doctored your coffee."

"Well, it looks like we're in the middle of nowhere without a horse or a gun." Birch pointed out several sets of hoof prints. "I suggest we start following them and hope like hell that there's a town somewhere within the next twenty miles or so."

CHAPTER 8

BY midday in northern Nevada Territory, the sun was beating relentlessly down on Birch and Tisdale. There was no cover or shelter for them, and with no transportation other than their feet, it was slow going—slower going with an injured Tisdale.

Birch looked over at his companion. Tisdale was noticeably more pale and Birch considered stopping again for a rest. He had stopped frequently because Tisdale had lost some blood and was weak.

As if reading Birch's mind, Tisdale fixed him with a steel-eyed glint and said firmly, "I hope you're not going to tell me we need to stop again, Birch. I could go on for another couple of miles."

Birch looked dubiously at Tisdale, noting the ashen color of his face and the sheen of perspiration on his forehead. Glancing down, Birch also took in the wobble in Tisdale's knees as he pressed on, determined not to let a little thing like a bullet wound and loss of blood affect him. He had to admire the man's fortitude.

"Look, Mr. Tisdale, I think we need to stop for a short while so you can rest up."

"I don't need rest, thank you very much," Tisdale snapped. "What I need is a town with a doctor in it who can give me something for the—" Here, Tisdale stopped and winced, muttering, "Hurts like the blazes."

Having been wounded before, Birch empathized with Tisdale. He guessed that this was the first time Tisdale had ever been shot. Lucky he was only grazed or he might have been carrying a bullet in him, Birch thought. Of course, the fact that neither of them had eaten a thing all day was affecting Tisdale's strength as well.

Birch looked around for something, anything, to eat, but he wasn't familiar enough with this harsh land to determine what was edible. Sage and bitter brush surrounded them. Off in the distance, Birch caught a glimpse of the Humboldt. They were coming back to the river and would be able to at least get some water. Birch wished that he were one of those men who could live off the land. Maybe then he would recognize something edible that would boost Tisdale's flagging energy.

As if his wish had been answered, Birch spotted something, someone, moving down by the Humboldt. Almost without thinking, he sped up, hoping to encounter a traveler or a miner who might share some food.

He could hear Tisdale's labored breath behind him, trying to keep up.

"Birch, wait for me!" Tisdale puffed.

Over his shoulder, Birch called, "There's someone down there by the river. A man with a horse! I'm going to try and catch up with him." With that, Birch broke into an easy run.

As he drew nearer, Birch realized that the man he'd seen from a distance was an Indian. From his days as a Texas Ranger, Birch could distinguish an Apache from a Comanche, but he wasn't sure what tribes inhabited such an inhospitable environment as the high desert plains of the Nevada Territory.

The Indian wore cured skins with little in the way of bead decorations. A small inverted basket covered his head like a hat, and long thin black hair sprouted from underneath, covering the man's shoulders.

Sensing Birch's presence, the Indian looked up from watering his horse. A sharply pointed stick rested at his side, but he made no hostile move with it. A mildly curious look crossed the strange-looking Indian's sun-brown face.

Tisdale caught up with Birch, weariness creasing his pale

face. He seemed to brighten a bit as he studied the Indian. "Paiute," he muttered. "Desert dweller."

"I've heard of desert Indians," Birch said in a low voice, "but I've never come face to face with one."

"They're not hostile like the Indians you knew back in Texas," Tisdale explained. "I know a little Indian sign language. Maybe I could ask him . . ."

The Paiute had turned toward the river as if the two crazy white men with no horse between them no longer interested him. He was bent over the river, peering into the water. Slowly he raised his sharp stick, took careful aim, then threw the weapon skillfully into the water. When he withdrew it, two fat trout were wriggling on the end of it.

Birch heard Tisdale's stomach growl. Apparently, so had the Paiute, for he turned around with a friendly look on his face and held the fish out toward the two men, making it clear that he was asking them to share his catch.

While the Paiute cleaned the trout, Birch made a fire from the kindling that their host had already gathered.

While they waited for their meal to cook, Tisdale attempted to tell the Paiute man what had befallen them. When he paused in his silent storytelling to search for the correct sign, the Indian would nod encouragingly to let him know that he was understood. Birch watched, fascinated by Tisdale's knowledge of signing.

As Tisdale neared the part where Johnston and Emma had escaped and how they were following on foot in an effort to recapture the accused man, the Paiute became animated. With a little effort, Tisdale translated his signs for Birch.

"He says that they passed this way about two hours ago." Tisdale hesitated. "I think he's telling us that they were heading toward a town which lies just about ten miles down the river."

Birch frowned. "That's only a few hours from here on foot."

"We should leave as soon as we eat, then."

Birch agreed. Fish had never been a favorite of his, but he had to admit that he'd never tasted freshly caught trout before. And the fact that he was very hungry might have had something to do with how delicious it was.

The Paiute also offered them some wild seeds, berries, and cooked roots from a few pouches that rested at his hip. With such variety, the simple meal of trout turned into a feast.

Afterward, they rested by the river with their host. He told Birch in gestures, translated by Tisdale, that he was return-ing to his family from a foraging excursion. Looking at the horse, Birch noticed, for the first time, the small travois hitched to the animal. A large basket, with a leather strap for slinging across his back, rested on the ground next to the horse. The basket was filled with roots, seeds, and wild berries. Strapped to the travois were several small animals hunted for their meat and their hides.

After an hour's rest, Birch noticed several dark clouds moving slowly toward them in the distance.

"We'd better get started," he told Tisdale.

Tisdale in turn pointed to the clouds and told their Indian host of their desire to move on before they were caught in the rain. After thanking the Paiute, they moved on, leaving their host to start his own trip back to his family.

"I'm impressed," Birch said after a while.

"What impressed you?" Tisdale asked mildly. His color had improved. The food and the rest had probably done as much for his condition as any doctor could do.

"I had no idea you knew sign language."

Tisdale smiled, continuing to look straight ahead, intent on getting to the town ten miles away. "I picked it up when I was in the army. I'm just fortunate I recalled enough to converse with our host. I had very little chance to use it while in the military."

Birch chuckled. "We were damn lucky to run into that

Paiute. I don't know how much longer we could have lasted without the food."

"We would have done perfectly fine. I know how to forage and fish," Tisdale replied shortly.

"Yeah, you could have saved us both," Birch said jokingly. *You looked like you were at death's door,* he thought.

He hoped the town was where that Indian said it was. Maybe Johnston and Emma felt they'd put enough miles between the campsite and the town. They might feel secure enough to stop there overnight.

They fell into an easy silence as the miles disappeared beneath their feet. Tisdale matched Birch's pace with seemingly little effort. Birch felt confident that the bullet wound must be on the mend.

Soon the sky darkened, not with the promise of nightfall, but with rain clouds. A few light drops began to fall, spattering the dry and dusty ground, covering the two men's hats and clothes with a fine mist.

Birch began looking around for some sort of shelter from the turn in the weather, but found nothing suitable as they continued moving forward.

As they crested an incline, Tisdale saw it first.

"Our Paiute friend was right," he declared, pointing toward a small drab settlement less than a ten-minute walk from where they stood.

Birch nodded silently, looking back at the land they had so recently crossed. The rain suddenly increased and the two men looked briefly at each other before hurrying toward the oasis.

CHAPTER 9

THE flat little town of Toy appeared empty when Birch and Tisdale approached it. They ducked into the first building they came to. They were soaked to the skin from the downpour, but a blast of hot air greeted them from a roaring hot open oven in the center of the room.

The steady clang of the smithy's mallet pounding metal into shape came from the other side of the room. The heat from the fire was so intense that it was difficult for Birch and Tisdale to see the man on the other side of it.

The blacksmith must have sensed that he was not alone, because the din stopped and he came out from behind his furnace. As with most metal workers, his arms bulged with muscles made strong from constant use. The rest of him was less impressive: short, bald, bearded, and his small frame carried an enormous potbelly.

"What can I do for you gentlemen?" he asked. His voice was friendly, but underlying it was the tone of a man wary of strangers. Especially wet, bedraggled strangers.

Birch replied, "We're looking for a doctor."

The blacksmith eyed Tisdale's sling, and he relaxed and nodded. "You'll want to see Red Haney, the town doctor. He's three buildings down on your right. Go to the side door. That's where he keeps his office."

Birch thanked him and they followed the blacksmith's directions to the doctor's building.

A tall, thin red-haired man with wire-rim bifocals answered the door. He turned out to be Doc Haney, and wasn't busy at the moment. Peeling Tisdale's shirt away from the bullet wound, Doc Haney checked the skin around the hurt area. Tisdale winced.

"Ayep. It's not too bad. If you've lived this long, you'll be all right," the doctor gruffly pronounced. "But you can't use this arm for a while now."

He cleaned the wound out with alcohol, dressed it, and fixed up a more acceptable sling. While Tisdale was settling up for the visit, Birch asked the doctor if he'd seen a man and woman ride into town.

"They were last seen heading this way. He's about six feet tall with sandy hair, about twenty-four years old. The woman has dark wavy hair and is a bit younger. They would have ridden into town, leading another horse."

Doc Haney looked thoughtfully at both men, considering Birch's question. After a long pause, he replied, "I'm afraid I can't help you much. I've been in my office most of the day."

They walked over to the stable, where Tisdale bought two horses outfitted with saddles.

"This is turning out to be the most expensive business trip I've ever taken," he said in a dry tone.

Birch smiled grimly. This whole assignment was not just a strain on Tisdale's pocketbook, but on Birch's pride. He wanted to get Johnston back into his custody, despite his continued belief in the kid's innocence. Johnston had had a perfect opportunity to rob Tisdale when Emma shot him and the fact that he didn't was one more reason why Birch believed the young man was not really an outlaw. But he knew Tisdale did not share this view of Johnston and had no interest in the case beyond earning the bounty for delivering Johnston.

Birch said, "I hope you have enough money to buy us some supplies, Mr. Tisdale."

With a frown, Tisdale replied, "So do I."

They led their horses to the general store. By then, it had stopped raining, but the main street was muddy with big puddles dotted here and there. Birch called a halt to their procession and pointed to a saloon next to the general store.

"Let's stop in there first. I need a drink."

Tisdale agreed wholeheartedly. Leaving their horses on the hitching post, they went inside and ordered a bottle of whiskey. They sat at one of the well-worn tables.

"Why don't we stay here tonight. There's a hotel across the street," Tisdale suggested. "We could get a good sleep and start out early tomorrow."

Birch shook his head and said, "You can if you want to, but I'm moving on as soon as I get some provisions for the trail. It's likely that Johnston and Emma will feel the same way you do and stop overnight, either in a town or camped out somewhere under the stars. I'm willing to bet it'll be the next town. We could overtake them by morning if we ride through the night."

Tisdale stared at his agent, clearly pleased with Birch's response. "I hope you're not just saying that to impress me, Birch. But even if you are, I am proud of you."

Birch looked away, annoyed. He hated the condescending tone Tisdale sometimes used, but tried to accord Tisdale the same respect he had shown to his former Ranger captain. Finally, Birch looked back, trying to keep his expression impassive as he said, "I say what I mean."

"You're very determined. No wonder you're so successful in completing assignments. Where will I ever find more men like you?"

Birch felt his good humor returning. He grunted and replied, "Worry about the agency later. Right now we've got more immediate concerns."

Tisdale looked curiously at Birch and asked, "Why are you so interested in catching Clem Johnston? From the way you interrogated that boy, I half got the impression that you thought he was innocent." He drained his drink in one gulp.

Birch poured another drink for them both and said, "I still think so. I can't think of a weaker reason to kill your boss than a week-old argument over the price of a new saddle deducted from your pay."

"He could have been lying," Tisdale pointed out.

"He could have. But somehow, I doubt it. Another reason I think he's not guilty is that when I was tracking him down, he could have shot me, but he shot wide on purpose."

"You can tell when someone does that? Maybe he was just a bad shot."

Birch shook his head again. "I don't think so. He had a chance to kill me when I was hanging from a ledge below him, but he shot into the air instead to scare me off."

Tisdale, looking dubious, said, "That seems like pretty thin evidence to me."

Birch shrugged. "It's not much, but there is another reason I'm starting to believe him."

"What's that?"

"He's heading southwest. We've been following a trail that will eventually lead right to Carson City."

Tisdale was silent as he thought that one over. After a while, he replied, "Perhaps the man has a less than keen sense of direction. Besides, if Clem Johnston is innocent, who killed Ashton?"

Birch smiled slightly and tossed his whiskey back. "I guess we'll just have to find out, won't we?"

Two rough-looking men walked in, ordered, and sat down at a nearby table. The smaller of the two looked mean, probably because he was squinting. The taller one wore a bushy unkempt beard and a shapeless hat perched on his balding head. Both of the men's clothes were filthy, as if they spent a good deal of their time outside, and the stench indicated that they didn't consider bathing a necessary experience.

"What do we do now?" Tisdale asked Birch.

"We've got our horses, we get some general store supplies and ask a few people if they've seen our friends."

Tisdale frowned. "What if people don't tell you what you want to know?"

Birch felt the corner of his mouth tug in amusement as he replied, "Well, I don't torture them, if that's what you're thinking. Hell, I don't even have a gun right now. I'll just keep asking until someone has seen them and tells me which way they're headed."

"But you said they're heading toward Carson City," Tisdale argued.

Birch allowed himself a smile this time. "There's always the possibility that I'm wrong and that Clem Johnston and Emma have doubled back or taken a new direction. I just want to confirm my own suspicions."

Tisdale nodded. Birch suggested that since Tisdale had the money, he get the supplies at the general store and also describe their quarry to the clerk. Meanwhile, Birch would ask here at the saloon. Between them, they'd find the necessary information.

Tisdale finished his drink and stood up to leave.

"Mr. Tisdale," Birch addressed him. Tisdale turned around. "We could use a gun."

He reached down, plucked a bullet out of his gunbelt, and tossed it to his employer. Tisdale caught it, then turned it around, examining it thoroughly.

Birch explained, "Try to buy a gun that takes that bullet. Then you won't need to buy a box of bullets."

Tisdale nodded. Then he turned and left.

Birch nursed his whiskey for a few more minutes before crossing the room. The bartender was surreptitiously sipping from a glass, but when he saw Birch approaching, he put the drink away, straightened up, and starting polishing the stained bar surface.

"Want another bottle?" he inquired in a gruff voice.

Birch shook his head. "I'm looking for a man and a woman who may have passed through your town earlier today. Or they may still be here."

The bartender looked up, a glint of greed in his eyes. "Is there anything in it for me?"

"Nothing but the knowledge that you helped catch an accused murderer," Birch replied mildly. He went on to describe Clem Johnston and Emma, but the bartender had lost interest once he discovered there was no reward.

When Birch turned back and started for his table, he noticed the two rough-looking men eyeing him belligerently.

Just as he reached his table, the smaller man, who wore a red shirt, got up and grabbed Birch's half-full whiskey bottle.

"Excuse me," Birch said, "but I paid for that."

The one with the bushy beard stood beside his companion and said, "That's not the way we see it. You left your table with the bottle on it."

"Yeah," said Red Shirt. He had a thin, whiny voice. "You left it there and we figured you'd left it for good."

"But you saw me walking back to my table just now." Birch couldn't stop himself from arguing. He was getting tired of being pushed around. He was also very aware that he wasn't wearing a gun at the moment, so he tried to keep the accusation out of his voice. "You came over for the bottle as I was returning."

Bushy Beard stepped forward menacingly. "Are you saying that we're trying to pick a fight with you?"

"That's the way it appears," Birch replied mildly, just before he sucker-punched the big man. Bushy Beard doubled over and staggered away to be sick in a nearby spittoon.

Red Shirt broke the whiskey bottle and waved the jagged edges in Birch's face, a mean look in his eye. The sickly smell of vomit and whiskey mingled. Red Shirt circled Birch, brandishing the broken bottle in front of him.

Birch grabbed a nearby chair and sideswiped Red Shirt with it. The whiskey bottle fell and rolled toward a corner of the room. Red Shirt staggered into a table, but righted himself and came at Birch, who ducked his first punch but was knocked on the side of his face with Red Shirt's other fist. Birch got another blow in, then they moved in close to each other and tangled, but neither got any punches in.

The bartender was apparently staying out of it, but soon Birch felt himself being torn away. Bushy Beard had recovered and gotten a full-nelson hold on Birch from behind. Birch tried to twist away, but Bushy Beard's grip was too strong. He reached up with both hands, the only direction that he could move his arms, and tried to tear his adversary's hands away from the back of his neck.

Meanwhile, Birch took three punches to his gut from Red Shirt. He decided to concentrate on putting the antagonist in front of him out of commission. Shifting his weight to his shoulders and using Bushy Beard's hold as leverage, Birch brought his legs up and, with his boots, pushed Red Shirt back across the room before the man got another punch in.

Bushy Beard must have been surprised, because he slackened his grip. Birch dug an elbow into his captor's gut and slipped his arms out of Bushy Beard's loose hold.

The big man doubled up, holding his stomach and groaning. Birch took the opportunity and gave him an uppercut to the jaw, sending him over a table. Bushy Beard didn't get up this time. But Red Shirt was coming back for him, a menacing look in his eyes. His hand hovered over his gun.

Birch held up his hands and said, "I'm not carrying a gun. If you shoot me, it'll be murder."

Red Shirt hesitated and in that moment, Birch dove for him, tackling him at the knees. They tumbled backward onto open floor space, and Birch sat atop the smaller man, bunching his shirt front in his grip. He couldn't resist getting a punch in, his fist connecting with the man's right cheekbone. It probably hurt Birch's hand more than it hurt his victim.

"Now what was this all about?" Birch demanded. "Do you boys just go after any stranger who happens through your town, or was this personal?"

A thin trickle of blood ran down Red Shirt's cheek, and his

breath came out in ragged gasps. Much to Birch's satisfaction, his right eye was beginning to swell shut.

"You were askin' around about the lady. She said you and your friend was outlaws that attacked her an' the man she's with."

Birch tightened the grip on his shirt, making it more difficult for him to breathe. "My friend and I are not outlaws. That lady's companion is wanted for murder down in Carson City and she helped him escape from me last night." Birch's tone became sharper. "Now you can either help me out by giving me the information I want, or I can haul you and your friend over to the marshal's office for a little visit, and we can tell him the whole story."

Bushy Beard had recovered, but wasn't making any hostile moves toward Birch. In fact, he said, "Better tell him what he wants to know, Zeb. I ain't spendin' no time in the pokey just on account of a lady."

Zeb sighed and tried to get more comfortable in Birch's grip. When he finally gave up on that, he told Birch, "They came in early this mornin' and went over to Miss Lil's for some grub. Me and Zack sat at a table next to 'em. She started talkin' to us and told us her story."

Zack sighed. "We believed her. She was so pretty. Don't see many young girls around these parts."

Birch eyed them both, then dropped his hold on Zeb. "Yeah, I guess you don't."

He got up slowly, his knees protesting being pressed against the hard wooden floor for so long. His hat had come off in the fight, and he picked it up and brushed it off before putting it back on.

Zack helped Zeb up and, with wary looks at Birch, they started for the door.

Birch stopped them with another question. "Which way were they headed?"

Zack relaxed and got a funny look on his face. "Now that

you mention it, they were headed southwest. Carson City is down there, ain't it?"

Birch nodded to his retreating back.

The bartender spoke up. "Hey! Who's going to pay for this mess?"

Tisdale came in at that moment, silently signaling to Birch that the supplies were ready.

Birch adjusted his hat and fixed the bartender with an appraising stare. If he'd been any help at all in answering Birch's questions or breaking up the fight, Birch might have been inclined to point to Tisdale. As it was, he said, "You know where to get ahold of those two who just left, don't you?"

The bartender nodded mutely.

"Well then, put it on their bill."

With that, Birch walked out of the saloon and joined Tisdale on the ride out of Toy.

CHAPTER 10

EMMA eased back on the reins of her dapple gray just outside of a small town called Hazen. Clem had been talking about stopping here for the night and renting a room. She argued they should be a little more cautious and stay away from towns. And if they absolutely had to get some supplies, she could go in by herself. But Clem had gotten it into his head that he was safe now.

"We could go on for another twenty-five miles, maybe thirty," she pointed out. "And we have bedrolls and food enough for tonight and tomorrow morning. Why take a chance that you might be recognized or that Birch might catch up to us?"

"I don't want to spend another night outdoors," Clem replied stubbornly. "It gets cold in the mountains this time of year, and I want to sleep in a bed with a pillow and have someone to cook my breakfast in the morning. For the past few nights, I've been curled up in damp cells on hard cots and on even harder ground with my wrists manacled to a tree. I tell you, I won't set up camp again, not if I can help it."

Exasperated, Emma said, "But you might be recognized. Besides, what if Birch and his friend reached Toy? What if they found horses and are heading this way right now?"

Clem looked very tired all of a sudden. "Maybe this wasn't such a good idea after all, Em. I really appreciate your help, but I think I should have just gone back to Carson City in Birch's custody. At least he didn't dismiss my story when I told it."

She sighed, a growing dread forming in the pit of her

58

stomach. Whenever she had this feeling, something awful happened soon after.

"Well, Clem, if we stop here, you might be recaptured by Birch," she said with a shrug and forced a smile, "but maybe nothing will happen after all. Let's see if there's a rooming house in town."

They rode into Hazen and were given directions to the only boardinghouse in town. It was a large weathered clapboard building with a porch that ran the length of the front and there was a swing on one side.

The woman who ran the guest house, Mrs. Flanagan, met them on the porch. A large woman in her fifties with a rosy complexion, she cast her eyes dubiously over their torn and dirty appearance. Her iron gray hair was pulled back in a bun at the nape of her neck, and she wore a starched white apron over her dress. Clem immediately turned on his charm, and before Emma could become discouraged, Mrs. Flanagan had taken a shine to Clem and told them she had two rooms for rent.

"We'll take them both," Clem said.

Emma frowned, turned to Mrs. Flanagan, and said, "Excuse me, do you mind if I talk to my companion privately for a moment?"

Mrs. Flanagan threw a motherly smile at Clem and said, "Of course. Just don't take too long to decide. I have to know how many boarders will be at the supper table."

Emma nodded and dragged a protesting Clem off to the porch swing.

"Clem, what are you thinking of?"

He looked at her strangely and replied, "What are you talking about?"

"One room. We only need one room, not two," she said, feeling like she was talking to a child. "We need to save our money."

"Emma"—Clem shook his head, stubborn as a mule on a

bad day—"it wouldn't be right, you and me in the same room."

Halfheartedly, Emma argued a little more, but she knew that when Clem made up his mind about something, it was difficult to get him to see the other side. In the end, Clem paid for the rooms.

"I think you'll be comfortable in both rooms," Mrs. Flanagan said as she showed them upstairs. "Where are you folks coming from? "

Clem and Emma's eyes met for an instant. They hadn't thought about the inevitable questions.

Emma responded first. "Oh, a little town you've probably never heard of in Oregon Territory." She rushed on before Mrs. Flanagan could question them more closely. "We're heading for Sacramento to visit my brother and look for work. We're thinking of settling there."

Mrs. Flanagan nodded indulgently. "I see. You're a young couple moving west. I must say, there's more work to be had in northern California now than there used to be." She paused at the door of the first room and said, "Here you are."

Emma slipped in, and with a polite smile and a thank you, she closed her door. From the hall, she could hear Clem telling Mrs. Flanagan that they weren't yet married, hence explaining the separate rooms.

Emma's was a pleasant little room with plain, whitewashed walls. The four-poster bed had a high feather mattress that was covered with a cheery homemade quilt and a large goosedown pillow. Emma had to admit that this room was luxurious compared to last night. She poured water into a basin from a matching jug and cleaned up a bit. Emma didn't have anything in the way of baggage to unpack, so when she felt she was presentable, she slipped out of her room to find Clem.

It wasn't difficult to find his room. Clem's door was ajar and he was seated in a rocking chair, gazing out of his window. She knocked on the door and he gestured for her to come in.

"Why?" she asked. "Finding that money in Birch's saddlebag was a stroke of luck, but we should be saving it."

Clem got up and lay down on his bed, tucking his arms under his head, and crossing his boots. He frowned and said, "We can always sell Sweet Betsy if we need more money. Why do you keep saying that we should save it?"

Sighing, Emma explained patiently, "For you to get away from here."

Clem propped himself up on one elbow and shrugged with the other. "What are you talking about?" he asked. "I thought we agreed last night."

"You agreed," she replied gently. Emma sat beside him, and placed a comforting hand on his shoulder. "Oh, Clem. The risk is too great. I don't want to lose you. Please reconsider. I know you didn't kill Frank Ashton, and you know it. What anyone else thinks doesn't matter."

Emma stole a glance in his direction. There was a dark expression on his face. He said in a low voice, "It does matter. It matters to me. I want to prove to everyone that I'm innocent, or I'll die trying."

Emma stood up, pacing and gesturing as she pleaded with him. "We could get far away from here and start over. You could get a job down south, maybe in Arizona Territory. I could find some work also . . ."

Clem stopped her with a sharp look. When he was angry, he usually stayed silent and brooded, which unnerved Emma. But this time, he spoke. "Em, you've done a lot more for me than I have any right to expect. Don't ever think I'm not grateful. But I have to set this right. I can't run away and spend the rest of my life wondering when someone will recognize me and hang me for a crime I didn't commit. I have to go back to Carson City."

The tears came then, and she felt as if her heart were falling down an endless black pit. "But you're all the family I have, Clem. Without you . . . ," she sobbed, unable to finish her sentence.

Clem clumsily patted her shoulder and wiped away her tears with his handkerchief.

When Emma had calmed down a bit, Clem said, "Maybe it would be better if you didn't go with me the rest of the way. Maybe you should stay here or go south without me. Start a new life. There could be trouble for you back in Carson City."

She stuck out her chin stubbornly. "If you're going back there, I'm going with you. Don't even think about leaving without me tomorrow morning, Clem Johnston, or— or . . ."

He smiled wearily. "We'll see. Let's not talk about this anymore today. Just enjoy the rest of the day and we'll discuss this tomorrow morning at breakfast."

Emma felt a little better. At least she'd have another chance to talk some sense into him in the morning. She forced herself to get up and cross the room, with the intention of leaving.

"Where are you going?" he asked.

She turned around gracefully, holding her skirt out. "To buy a new dress," Emma replied lightly. "Did you see the suspicious look on Mrs. Flanagan's face when we paid for our rooms? I don't think she believed we had a penny between us! And I don't blame her—I look awful."

Clem looked skeptical. "This is a pretty small town, Em. Are you sure you can buy a dress around here?"

She shrugged. "I'll see what they have at the general store down the street. I'll settle for a new skirt and shirtwaist, anything." She indicated her torn skirt.

He nodded. "I have to take our horses over to the stable, so I guess I'll see you at supper."

Out in the hall, Emma leaned against the wall, feeling drained. She realized soon after she'd started talking to Clem that he wasn't going to change his mind. He'd gotten it into his head that he had to go back to Carson City and find the killer.

With a sigh, she left Mrs. Flanagan's boardinghouse to find a decent dress in this godforsaken town.

Emma came back several hours later with a new dress, a hairbrush and comb, gloves, and a light woolen shawl for cooler evenings. Mrs. Flanagan was just setting the table for supper.

She paused when she caught sight of Emma in the dining room doorway. "My, that's a pretty dress. A far sight better than what you were wearing earlier."

Emma blushed and fingered the cheery calico dress, a pattern of small blue and white flowers on a red background. She wasn't used to such bright colors, but it had been the only dress available.

"You should show off your new dress to your young man," Mrs. Flanagan advised in a smug tone.

"My young man?" Emma repeated.

"The young man who came here with you," the boarding-house owner reminded her. "He is your young man, isn't he?"

Before Emma could answer, Clem stepped into the room. "I hope so. You haven't forgotten me so soon, have you, dearest?" he asked with a wink.

Emma regained her composure. "Of course not."

Clem stepped back and looked at her in an appraising manner. "Turn around, Em."

She did so.

With an approving nod, he said, "You look nice. Red suits your hair and skin color."

"I'll be serving supper in about fifteen minutes," Mrs. Flanagan interrupted with a twinkle in her eye. "You might want to take your young lady out onto the porch swing until then."

Clem took Emma's arm and guided her onto the porch.

As they sat and swung slowly back and forth, Emma glanced over at Clem. He looked troubled. She broke the silence.

"What's bothering you?" she asked.

He twisted his mouth and stuck out his jaw, a habit he'd picked up a long time ago when he was brooding. Looking down at his hands, he said, "I was thinking about the knife again."

She sighed. "Do you have any ideas about who it might have belonged to?"

After thinking very hard for a few moments, Clem finally shook his head shortly, and frustration lacing his voice, said, "I *know* I've seen that knife somewhere before. Someone took it out to show everyone at the Harvest Dance. I was a little drunk at the time, and now every time I think I've almost remembered the name of the knife's owner, it slips away from me."

Without evincing much sympathy, Emma retorted, "A bottle of whiskey will do that to you, plays tricks on your memory."

Clem replied dryly, "Thank you, Mother."

For a moment, they forgot their troubles and grinned at each other. From the backdoor in the kitchen, the dinner bell sounded. Mrs. Flanagan was calling her boarders to supper.

Emma's stomach growled and she realized that she hadn't eaten since early that morning. She and Clem went inside. The rest of the night passed without incident. She dutifully played Clem's sweetheart whenever Mrs. Flanagan or one of the other boarders addressed her.

Emma slept poorly that night. She dreamed about their escape the night before, but whenever Emma and Clem thought they'd gotten away, she would turn around and find Jefferson Birch pursuing them mercilessly. She looked around for somewhere to hide, but no place was big enough for both herself and Clem. Finally, she screamed, "Save yourself, Clem. Run away! Hide!" But Clem just stood there staring at a giant Birch.

With the sun streaming through the lace curtains in her room, Emma woke up early. Maybe today she could convince Clem to ride in another direction.

After donning her red dress and combing out the tangles in her dark hair, she stepped out of her room and knocked on Clem's door. No answer.

He must be downstairs already, Emma thought. She went downstairs to the dining area. Mrs. Flanagan and one of the boarders were seated at the table with full plates. The boarder, a middle-aged man who hadn't yet said a word in her presence, was now staring at her. When she met his eyes, he dropped his gaze and concentrated on his breakfast again.

Mrs. Flanagan looked up at Emma, stark pity in her eyes.

"My, dear," she exclaimed, "why don't you sit down and have something to eat!"

Emma looked around. "Where's Clem?" she asked. "Has he had breakfast yet?"

Mrs. Flanagan stood up, her hands wringing a lacy hand-kerchief. After a moment's hesitation, she came forward and put a hand on Emma's arm.

"My dear," she started gently, hesitated, then continued, "Your young man has gone off."

"What are you talking about?" Emma asked numbly.

Mrs. Flanagan started again. "He had breakfast over an hour ago and told me that you were both leaving today. Then he strolled over to the stable to check the horses." She paused, then said, "It was terribly early. I didn't think the stable would be open yet."

Emma remained silent. She couldn't think of anything to say.

Mrs. Flanagan guided her young boarder to a chair and sat her down before continuing, gesturing with a hand to the male boarder at the table. "Mr. Benson here was taking a morning walk, as is his habit. He saw your young man riding out of town about an hour ago."

"Why don't you eat something," Mrs. Flanagan again urged, patting her hand. "You can stay here as long as you need to."

Emma nodded. While Mrs. Flanagan was in the kitchen getting a plate, Emma turned to Mr. Benson.

"Was he leading two other horses or was he riding just one?" she asked.

He chewed his food thoughtfully and finally replied, "Just the one."

She thanked him for the information. Clem was clever. He knew she'd follow him. But he hadn't waited around for her, probably because he knew she'd try to discourage him again from heading for Carson City. Another reason occurred to her—if he was caught in Carson City before he could find the killer, she wouldn't be accused of aiding a criminal.

She ate little, leaving most of her breakfast untouched. Then she went back to her room to gather the few things she'd bought in Hazen. She'd be on her way soon.

Suddenly she wondered whether Jefferson Birch would have notified the Carson City marshal that she had aided in Clem Johnston's escape. Or maybe Birch and Tisdale were still trying to catch up with them. Had Birch figured out that they were heading back to Carson City yet? He was a determined man and with his experience, she was certain Jefferson Birch and his colleague Tisdale would have no problem following their trail.

A warm feeling came over her at the thought of Birch. She tried to brush away the feeling, angry with herself for being attracted to the man who was trying to take Clem back to Carson City to face trial. There wasn't an iota of doubt in her mind that Clem was innocent.

The thought of going back to Carson City was a prospect that filled Emma with dread. She wasn't sure what kind of reception she'd get from the law and the townspeople if she returned. But she was resigned to the fact that while her future was uncertain, Clem might not *have* a future when he returned to Carson City.

CHAPTER 11

BIRCH and Tisdale had ridden hard from Toy to Hazen, at least a fifty-mile ride. The terrain didn't change much. Sagebrush swept otherwise barren plains for miles, and hazy mountains rose up in the distance on either side of the two men as they urged their horses on in silence. Occasionally, they caught glimpses of the Humboldt River.

Twice along the way, they had stopped to water their horses and had eaten the hardtack and jerky that Tisdale had bought at the general store in Toy. Birch occasionally drew the Smith & Wesson out of his holster, hefting its unfamiliar weight in his hand. He wasn't sure how good a shot he'd be with this new gun—Birch was used to the smooth-handled grip of his Navy Colt.

"How much farther are we going on this fool's journey?" Tisdale asked Birch.

Determination in his voice, Birch answered, "As far as we have to go. Until we find Clem Johnston or reach Carson City. Whichever comes first." Birch thought he detected a slight reluctance on Tisdale's part. Birch added reassuringly, "We'll find him, Mr. Tisdale. Before we reach Carson City."

Birch urged his horse on, leaving Tisdale in the dust.

They rode through the night until the sun began to peak through distant hills. Both men were exhausted, and Birch was about to call out for another rest when Tisdale caught a glimpse of lights in the distance.

"That must be a town. Maybe they stopped there," Tisdale said, unable to keep the exhaustion mixed with hope out of his voice. "Let's find out."

Birch was silent, but he spurred Cactus in that direction.

When they arrived, the town was starting to wake up. Hazen was bigger than Toy, but not by much. There were two saloons instead of one, a hotel, and a boardinghouse. And there was a telegraph office. Which was still closed. Birch had hoped to send a wire to the Carson City marshal, but it would have to wait until tomorrow. Maybe he'd have Clem Johnston in custody by then.

They reached the stables just as the owner was opening his doors. Birch figured that if Clem Johnston and Emma were in town, they might have boarded their horses here.

"Did you board any horses last night?" Birch asked.

The man looked at Birch with suspicion. "I might have," he answered evasively. Birch began to move toward the stalls and the man protested, "Hey! You can't just walk in here and—"

Shaking off the stable owner's hand on his arm, Birch stopped halfway down the row and stared into a stall.

Tisdale paused next to him and followed his gaze. He asked, "Is that your horse?"

Birch nodded silently.

The stable owner glared at them. "What's the problem, mister?"

Birch shook himself out of his trance and addressed the man. "How long has this horse been boarded here?"

The man rubbed his whiskered chin. "Well, now. Seems I can't remember."

Birch prompted Tisdale with a look. Reluctantly, Tisdale reached into his pocket and thrust a silver dollar into the owner's hand.

The man squinted at the dollar, bit it, and examined it again. When he was satisfied that it was indeed silver, he pocketed it and answered Birch's question. "I took the horse in late yesterday with a couple of other horses."

"The man who brought this horse in, what did he look like?"

The stable owner drew back, his friendly manner turning into suspicion. "Say, what's this really about?"

Tisdale intervened, explaining their interest in a soothing manner. "We think we recognize this horse. It belongs to my brother, and it may have been stolen."

Birch wondered at Tisdale's evasion, but went along with it. He'd get an explanation as soon as they were away from here.

The stable owner's expression relaxed and he nodded. "Well, actually, it was this young man who came in. He had several horses with him. There's one of the other horses he brought in." He pointed to Sweet Betsy in a nearby stall.

While the stable owner hadn't mentioned an accompanying woman, Birch supposed that Johnston and Emma had taken a room first and Johnston had gone over later, alone, to board the horses.

Birch was aware that Tisdale's horse wasn't pointed out by the stable owner, and he had a bad feeling that Johnston had eluded them again.

"Do you know where he's staying?" Birch asked, moving over to Cactus's stall and rubbing his nose affectionately.

Tisdale pressed two more coins into the stable owner's palm.

He must have trusted them at this point because he just pocketed the silver dollars instead of biting them first and said, "Over at Mrs. Flanagan's boardinghouse. At least that's where he said he was staying. Just turn left when you leave here and keep going till you come to a gray house with a swing on the porch. Only one in town."

Birch and Tisdale nodded, thanked him, and moved toward the door.

"But I wouldn't go over there now, if I was you," he called after them.

Birch turned and asked, "Why not?"

"Oh, Mrs. Flanagan's full up right now. And she's probably serving breakfast right now."

As they walked over to the rooming house, something kept nagging at Birch, but he couldn't quite put a finger on it at the moment. He rubbed his eyes, feeling the grit that accompanied a sleepless night.

Still, Birch couldn't get the idea out of his head that there was a chance Johnston had slipped through their fingers.

"Why did you lie to the stable owner back there?" Birch finally asked Tisdale.

His employer frowned and stroked his mustache. "Why should I tell him the truth? As I told you before, the law will pay a reward for Johnston's capture. I certainly don't want that blackmailer in the stables to get the money."

Birch was annoyed that it still came down to money for Tisdale. He was just as anxious to find Johnston and take him back to Carson City, and he certainly wouldn't mind getting paid for bringing him in. But he was also concerned about Johnston's safety. If the wanted man was going back home to find the killer, Clem Johnston probably would encounter plenty of men who wouldn't hesitate to kill him for the reward.

"How do you propose to apprehend a criminal, a murderer at that, at the breakfast table?" Tisdale asked.

Birch replied, "I don't think Johnston is a killer. I don't think he'll use a gun on us."

Tisdale frowned. "I'll remind you that Clem Johnston is wanted for murder. I don't think he'll feel any remorse about killing us." A pained expression crossed his face as he added, "And if not Johnston, his accomplice was certainly willing enough to take a shot at me."

Birch shook his head. "I don't think he's guilty. Why else would he be heading back to Carson City?"

"You mentioned that to me earlier but I still don't believe he's going there. He's trying to throw us off the trail."

Birch stubbornly stuck to his point. "He wants to go back and find the killer himself. So he won't hang for a crime he didn't commit."

"Again, I might remind you that the chances of finding Johnston innocent are pretty remote. He was found standing over Frank Ashton's body with the murder weapon in his hand."

"It's too convenient," Birch protested. It suddenly occurred to him what had been bothering him since Johnston had told his version of the Ashton killing, and he said to Tisdale, "There's something about the Ashton murder that I want to follow up on."

Tisdale shook his head and looked blank. "What are you talking about?"

Birch explained, "We need to talk to the people who saw Johnston in the barn. If he stabbed Frank Ashton, he'd have likely had a lot of blood on his shirt." When he'd been a Texas Ranger, Birch had seen enough stabbings to know that the killer's shirt had blood spatters on it afterward.

Tisdale studied Birch for a moment. "What does that prove?"

Birch replied, "If Johnston's clothes were clean, he's probably telling the truth. If there was blood on them, he most likely killed Frank Ashton."

They reached the boardinghouse, a big gray building with some attempts at a flower garden in the front. A large woman stepped out onto the porch. She wore her putty-colored hair pulled back in a severe style, and her florid complexion did not enhance the suspicious expression on her face.

In a voice as cold as steel, she asked, "Can I help you gentlemen? I was about to sit my boarders down to a morning meal."

Birch took his hat off and, in a humble tone, replied, "Excuse me, ma'am. We heard you cooked the finest breakfast in town and were wondering if you had room for two more."

When her face softened, Mrs. Flanagan looked almost pleasant. She said, "Well, as a matter of fact, there is room because one of my boarders just finished eating, and another left early this morning." She beckoned them in.

Birch stiffened at the news about someone having left, but hoped his feeling was wrong. A sidelong glance at Tisdale assured him that his employer also was worried that Johnston had got away. But they had to make sure he wasn't hiding in here first.

They followed Mrs. Flanagan inside. Cloying flowered wallpaper covered the hallway, parlor, and dining area. A large slablike table sat in the center of the room with eight chairs surrounding it. Savory aromas emanated from the kitchen door.

Several men sat around the dining table already. They looked up for a moment when Birch and Tisdale entered, but went back to their biscuits, sausage, gravy, eggs, grits, and steaming mugs of hot black coffee. Clem Johnston wasn't among them.

Birch glanced toward the stairs that led up to the rooms, wondering if he could slip away unnoticed to search them, but Mrs. Flanagan returned from the kitchen at that moment with two plates and set them down in front of two empty chairs. Birch and Tisdale slipped into spots at the table and began to eat.

Before long, however, the other boarders resumed their conversation, ignoring the new customers.

A man in his mid-thirties with a pale expression said, "I can't imagine what sort of scoundrel would leave a woman stranded in a strange town. With almost no money, I might add. I wonder what she'll do. He seemed in quite a hurry and looked like he didn't want to be recognized."

Birch almost choked on his biscuit. Frustration welled up in him. He was about to ask what they were talking about when Tisdale spoke.

"Excuse me," he asked in a tone of mild interest, "but could you please describe the people you're discussing?"

Mrs. Flanagan had sat down by now and gave him an

imperious look. "Excuse me, but I don't see what business it is of yours, sir."

Tisdale replied, "Oh, it might be of interest, ma'am. You see, my companion and I are searching for my sister." He gestured toward Birch, who glared at him. Unruffled, he added, "His wife. She ran away with a young man from our ranch a few weeks ago. We don't care about the man, but her three children do miss her."

Mrs. Flanagan's eyes teared up as she muttered, "Oh, those poor children."

Birch resigned himself to Tisdale's deception. If Johnston was gone anyway, telling the truth would just cause an uproar in the boardinghouse.

From Mrs. Flanagan's reaction, Birch knew that she had swallowed the story like a fish swallows a fishing hook. Looking around at the other boarders, he noticed that their expressions varied from dubious to disinterested. He doubted they would speak up or cause trouble.

Tisdale added solemnly, "Little Timothy, June, and young Brian are staying with my wife until we return with or without their mother."

He had reeled her in. With a determined look, Mrs. Flanagan crooked her finger and ordered, "Come with me."

She turned and marched through the dining room, the parlor, and into the hall, then ascended the stairway, Tisdale following. Birch brought up the rear, suddenly reluctant. What would he do when confronted with Emma? She would inevitably deny knowing them, perhaps even tell Mrs. Flanagan a lie similar to the one she had told that caused the fight in Toy.

However, looking back on Mrs. Flanagan's attitude before Tisdale told his story, Birch doubted he could have got this far with her by telling the truth.

Tisdale paused halfway up the stairs, perhaps sensing his agent's hesitancy. In a low voice, he told Birch, "If it's Emma, kiss her. I'll get rid of Mrs. Flanagan."

Birch nodded.

Mrs. Flanagan's imperious voice called out from the top of the stairs, "Gentlemen!"

They hurried up the remaining steps.

She stopped at a door on the left side of the hall and knocked. Birch was relieved that it didn't look out on the main street, so there was little chance Emma had seen their approach.

The door opened at the same time a familiar voice started to say, "I'm just packing up a few things, Mrs. Flanagan. Then I'll be—"

Birch needn't have worried about Emma getting a word in before he was able to do his part. She stopped and stared at the two men. Her jaw dropped open, leaving her speechless.

"Your husband and brother have come to fetch you home," Mrs. Flanagan said mistily. She dabbed at the corner of her eyes with a lace-edged handkerchief.

Emma blinked and started to speak. "But I'm not—"

"Darling!" Birch said, stepping forward and edging the weepy Mrs. Flanagan aside. He took the wide-eyed Emma in his arms and kissed her.

CHAPTER 12

EMMA struggled to push Birch away, but he wrapped his arms more tightly around her. She finally yielded to his vicelike grip.

Tisdale hissed in his ear, "She's gone. I've closed the door. You can stop now."

Birch relaxed. Emma twisted out of his embrace, eyes blazing, her cheeks flushed with indignation, and a furious expression on her face. She confronted the two men, apparently unsure of whom to address first. It didn't take her long to make up her mind. She turned to Birch and struck him.

The slap stung Birch's pride more than his cheek as his thoughts flashed back to accepting coffee from this devious woman two nights ago. He realized how fortunate they were to have found her in this place. Another fifteen minutes or so and she might have been gone. It still annoyed him that Clem Johnston had escaped his custody with the help of a woman.

"How dare you come in here!" she spat. "And lying to that nice woman . . ."

"Perhaps you'd prefer that we tell her the truth," Tisdale said pleasantly. He shifted his wounded shoulder for emphasis.

Emma opened her mouth to say something, then seemed to think better of it.

"I thought you'd enjoy a kiss from your long lost husband, Emma," Birch said dryly.

As if she suddenly realized her situation, Emma's face turned ashen. She turned away from Birch and Tisdale, and looked out the window, hugging her arms as if she were cold.

When she turned back to them, Emma appeared drained of her earlier defiant manner. She seemed almost contrite.

"I'm sorry I shot you." With her grave eyes fixed on Tisdale, Emma addressed him. "I'm not used to guns. It just went off. I'm relieved that you're still alive."

He nodded solemnly but said nothing, apparently waiting for Birch to initiate conversation.

Birch sighed wearily and said, "Where is Clem Johnston, Emma?"

She stared obstinately at him. He took a step toward her and she deftly backed up.

Birch held up a hand and asked mildly, "Do you think I'm going to beat an admission out of you? I've done a lot of unpleasant things in my life, but hitting a woman isn't one of them."

She seemed to relax slightly, but looked away from him.

Birch tried again. "Why are you protecting him, Emma? I don't have to be a fortune-teller to know where he's headed."

Emma looked sharply at him.

Birch continued, "He's heading back to Carson City, isn't he?"

Emma caught her breath and her eyes glittered with tears.

He added, "I know you love him, but you aren't helping him by remaining silent. Did he remember something that might lead him to the killer?"

She blinked and said slowly, "Then you believe him?"

Birch nodded.

Emma let out a sigh and her arms dropped to her sides as if she'd dropped all of her defenses. In a tired and distant voice, she said, "Clem is my half-brother, if you hadn't already guessed. He's the only family I have left."

Birch had not guessed; in fact, the true nature of her relationship to Johnston came as a surprise. Glancing at his employer, he noticed that Tisdale's eyebrows were raised.

Emma crossed the room, sat gingerly on the edge of the bed, and explained, "I've been trying to convince him to run from it all, but he's stubborn. Clem said he didn't want to have this murder hanging over his head for the rest of his days."

"If he did run," Birch replied, "there would always be a chance that someday someone would recognize him and he'd be taken back to stand trial. Or worse."

Straightening her shoulders, Emma nodded. "I guess you're right." For the first time since they'd been in the room together, Emma looked directly at Birch and said, "So what do we do now?"

"We could take you to the marshal in town and have him hold you in a cell for a few days until we found your brother."

She frowned at this suggestion and Birch continued, "Or we could join forces and look for Clem, then try to find the killer."

Her face brightened a bit, then turned cautious again.

"How do I know you're not trying to trick me into helping you find Clem?" she asked. "You might just be telling me what I want to hear, then you'll turn around and give Clem up to the law without even trying to find out the truth." She narrowed her eyes at the thought.

"You'll just have to trust me," Birch said simply. "I've told you what I know and what I think about Clem and the murder. I only know what he told me, but I don't think he had motive enough to kill Frank Ashton."

Tisdale stepped forward and said, "I can vouch for Birch's interest, Miss Johnston. He's been trying to convince me all along that your brother might be innocent."

Emma turned to him and asked, "And what do you think, Mr. Tisdale?"

Tisdale stroked his mustache thoughtfully and replied, "To be honest with you, Miss Johnston, I'm not sure. From what I had been told by the Carson City marshal and the Ashton family, I'm inclined to believe that Clem Johnston is guilty. But there's something to be said for Birch's reasoning."

Emma looked puzzled. "And what is that?"

Birch launched into his theory about the killer's clothing being bloodstained. When he'd finished, Emma's expression had become more animated.

"Oh, I wish I'd thought of that when Clem was around," she said with dismay, then added, "You know, he's been trying so hard to remember who owns that knife. Unfortunately, the only time he saw the knife before the killing, he'd been drinking heavily."

Birch said, "That would cloud his memory."

"Well?" Tisdale held his arms out, looking at Birch and Emma expectantly. "Are we going to stand here talking theories all day or are we heading for Carson City?"

Emma replied, "Let's go. I'm willing to believe you for now."

They said goodbye to Mrs. Flanagan. She was thrilled to have taken part in supposedly patching up their marriage. She stood on her front porch and waved her handkerchief after them.

"Go back to your three wonderful children and God bless you," she trilled as Birch, Tisdale, and Emma walked toward the stable.

"There's one thing I can't figure out," Birch said. "It's minor, but I like everything to have an explanation."

Emma asked, "What's that?"

"If Clem just left you this morning, and Mr. Tisdale and I walked over from the stable to the boardinghouse in search of you both, how did he manage to get away?"

Emma frowned, obviously concerned as well, but with no explanation forthcoming. She shook her head finally. "He must have seen you before you saw him, and stayed out of sight."

Birch and Tisdale nodded. When they got to the stable, the stable owner looked at them curiously.

"Howdy, folks, what can I do for you today?" He looked at

them closer and blinked in recognition. "Say, you're the two fellas who were just in here a little while ago."

"Yes," Birch said, "and I wanted to ask you—"

The stable owner went on as if he didn't hear Birch. "Yessir. That feller you was asking about rode out of here about an hour ago. But he only took one horse. He left yours. I told him you was pretty mad. He lit out of here like hell was on his heels."

Birch glanced at Emma. Her lips were tightly compressed into a thin line.

Tisdale was bursting with impatience. "For heaven's sake, man, why didn't you tell us this when we were here earlier?"

The man looked offended. "You didn't ask. 'Sides, I don't get paid to cause trouble for my customers. If I did, I'd be out of business. That's what the marshal's for. You shoulda gone to him with your troubles. He paid good money same as you. As long as he left your horse here, I didn't think it was any of your business if he left."

Tisdale drew an exasperated sigh and settled up their bill. Apparently Clem had only paid for the horse he took. Tisdale ended up paying for the remaining horses, Cactus and Sweet Betsy, plus the horses they'd bought back in Toy.

"You got an extra horse here," the man pointed out.

They hadn't reckoned with having this problem. Yesterday we had no horses, Birch thought wryly, and today, we have more than we can handle. In the end, the stableman reduced the boarding fee and kept Sweet Betsy for his children to ride.

With their horses saddled and ready to go, Birch, Emma and Tisdale headed south. Birch looked back once. The town of Hazen had grown so small that he felt he could reach out with his hand, pluck it up, and put it in his pocket.

CHAPTER 13

MY Navy Colt, my rifle, and my money are gone, but at least I have Cactus back, Birch thought as they started out for Carson City. Johnston had no doubt used the money up and taken the rifle and gun for protection.

He looked over at Tisdale and noticed that his shoulder didn't seem to be bothering him nearly as much as yesterday. Emma rode one of the horses bought in Toy, her red skirt riding up her shapely calves as she straddled the wide leather saddle.

Before they'd left Hazen, Tisdale had tried to convince Birch to wire ahead to Carson City, but with Emma looking on, Birch couldn't do it.

"You'd be doing the boy a favor, Birch," Tisdale warned. "He might run into the wrong people and get hurt when he gets back there."

"Clem can take care of himself," Emma's cold voice intervened. In a softer tone, she pleaded, "Please don't set up an ambush."

Birch was torn. Tisdale had a good point, but he wanted Emma's full cooperation. In the end, he decided to put off sending a wire. His reasoning was that Johnston had gotten an hour's head start. By the time the wire arrived in Carson City, chances were that he'd already have been captured.

It was a chance they would have to take. Birch had already accepted the fact that they wouldn't get the reward money. He was pretty sure that Tisdale was aware of this fact, too. If he wasn't, Birch wasn't in the mood to point it out to him. He'd gotten no sleep last night and was feeling a little edgy at the moment.

Tisdale appeared to accept, without further comment, Birch's decision not to wire ahead. He was surprised that Tisdale hadn't tried to use his authority to override the decision.

Along the trail south, Birch picked up a few signs that Clem Johnston, or possibly some other hard rider, had been this way recently. It was more likely to have been Johnston. Any other rider would have had to pass through Hazen on the way south.

Tisdale and Birch had left the Humboldt River back in Toy. The sage, chaparral, and scrub brush gave way to mountains and majestic pines. Birch was sure that the mountains would be covered with lush green vegetation if it were spring. But it was early fall, and the hills were dry and brown from the effects of the searing summer sun. This time of year the days were as hot as midsummer and the nights as chilly as early winter.

Birch could feel the day's warmth through his cotton shirt. Beads of sweat rolled down his spine and clung to his brow as he tried to make the most of every small breeze that blew. He would be glad to reach their destination and get something cold to drink.

By Birch's estimation, the ride to Carson City would take less than a day at the rate they were going. Emma didn't try to slow them down at all. Maybe the inevitability of it all had finally caught up with her and she'd come to realize that cooperation was the best way. On the other hand, Birch thought, maybe Emma was planning an unexpected escape as they neared Carson City so she could warn her brother.

He had to admire Emma for her courage and resolution. The only other woman he'd known recently with these qualities was Mattie Quinn, a widowed Montana ranch owner. When someone had tried to pressure her into selling her land by using scare tactics, she'd hired Birch to investigate. The last he'd heard from her, she'd married one of her ranch hands, named Omaha.

The sun was still high in the sky when Birch called for a rest. He could have gone on the rest of the way, but accompanying him were a woman, and a man recovering from a bullet wound. Besides, the day had turned hot, and Birch knew it wouldn't hurt to water the horses.

A small watering hole lay at the foot of a low hill, which was surrounded by a group of trees. Birch looked for signs that his escaped prisoner had been there, but the area around the water was so muddy from animal tracks that it obscured any possible sign of recent human use.

After they filled up their water bags, Tisdale insisted on taking charge of the horses while Birch and Emma stretched out in the cool shade.

Birch was enjoying the silence when Emma spoke up. "How long before we get to Carson City?"

"I've never been there, but Mr. Tisdale told me that the stagecoach trip up to Paradise Valley from Carson City took two days," Birch said. "Considering how close we are, I'd say we'll be there in a few hours if we keep up this pace."

"I'm worried about Clem," Emma confided. "I know what I did to you the other night was wrong, but he's my only kin. I don't want to lose him."

"Tell me," Birch said, suddenly interested, "how did you catch up with us? How did you know where to find Clem?"

She looked away at the hills. A cool breeze rippled the surface of the watering hole. Birch adjusted himself so the breeze would hit his back.

Finally she replied, "Clem came to me in Carson City the night after he escaped. I knew everyone was looking for him, so I followed my normal routine and went for a walk right before dinner. He called to me from an alley so no one would see me. I agreed to meet him up north in Pine Ridge a few weeks later. We thought it would be less obvious if I didn't go away immediately. He figured he could hide out until then."

"He didn't send a wire to you then," Birch said thoughtfully.

"That was what he'd planned on doing, but I told him that it would lead the law straight to him. As it turned out," Emma wasn't able to keep the bitterness out of her voice successfully as she continued, "you found him anyway."

Birch smiled slightly and reminded her, "But I'm not the law."

She shook her head. "You might as well be. Clem didn't have a chance from the moment he walked into the Ashtons' barn."

"You must have had time to think about what happened," Birch suggested, then continued, "but you've only answered half of my question. How did you know where to find us that night you came into our camp?"

She shrugged and answered readily enough. After all, it wasn't important anymore. "I was already in Pine Ridge and caught sight of you two heading out of town. I was desperate, so I took one of the horses tethered to a hitching post and followed your trail out of town. I just kept riding until I got to Paradise Valley. I recognized you coming out of the general store, so I registered at the hotel and stayed out of your sight.

"When you left the next morning," Emma continued, "I trailed behind you by a few miles until you made camp, then waited until it became dark before staggering into your camp."

"What about the horse you rode in on?"

She smiled apologetically and said, "I'd meant for us to find the horse in the morning, but it didn't work out that way. I hope someone found it."

Birch shook his head. He had to admire her for her bravery. "Stealing a horse is more serious in these parts than killing a man," he said. Seeing her look of dismay, he quickly added, "I'm sorry, but it's true. You're lucky you abandoned the horse when you did. Either the horse headed back home or the owner tracked it down, and since he'd gotten his property back, decided to abandon the search for the horse thief." Birch decided to change the subject. "Emma, do you have any ideas about who might have killed Frank Ashton?"

Emma laughed harshly. "Everyone. Anyone who had contact with Frank Ashton. I even have a motive. He made it clear that he wanted to be intimate with me. Every time I visited Clem, which wasn't often, Mr. Ashton would find an opportunity to be alone with me. He wouldn't take no for an answer."

Birch didn't blame the late Frank Ashton for being attracted to pretty Emma Johnston. But it was surely no reason to harass her.

Emma must have been reading his thoughts. "He was persistent with everyone," she offered. "He couldn't believe that some people like to be left alone. Ashton thought he could buy loyalty and affection from anyone when it was advantageous for him. He didn't understand that some people value their pride above financial gain."

"Had anyone fought with him recently? Does anyone's name come to mind, someone who might have more reason than normal to kill Frank Ashton?" Birch watched Emma's face change. She clearly thought this conversation was distasteful. He quickly reminded her, "Emma, if it weren't important, I wouldn't ask. I can understand that you might not want to point the finger at someone, but this is your brother's life we're talking about."

Tisdale tethered the horses to a nearby branch and entered the grove.

"What have I missed?" he asked, a curious expression on his face.

With a sinking heart, Birch glanced back at Emma. He wouldn't get any more information from her now that Tisdale was with them. She still didn't trust Tisdale.

I wonder how far she trusts me, Birch thought.

Emma replied shortly, "Nothing," in answer to Tisdale's question. She stood up and brushed imaginary dirt off her skirt. "Isn't it time we moved on?"

Birch sighed wearily and got to his feet, Tisdale following suit. Mounting the horses, they headed south at a fast clip.

Birch felt that he had nothing to go on. First he had offered to help Clem Johnston, then his sister Emma. Although both brother and sister gratefully accepted, neither one had been particularly forthcoming with information that might prove useful in investigating the Ashton killing. Knowing that almost everyone in Carson City was a candidate for Ashton's murderer wasn't narrowing down the list.

As they neared Carson City, Birch wondered how long it would take Emma Johnston to double-cross him in a vain effort to save her brother.

Emma slowed down at a fork in the trail. The main path was straight and wide, but a secondary road veered off to the east.

"The smaller road leads to the Ashton ranch," she explained. "You might want to start by asking some questions of the ranch hands who were working there at the time of the murder."

Birch nodded. "I will be doing that, but first I want to check with the marshal—"

"Check with the marshal?" she asked with alarm, her eyelashes fluttering. Skeptically, Emma added, "Why would you want to do that?"

"He might have some useful information," Birch explained.

Suspicion crept into her voice as she replied, "You're not going to tell him about Clem's escape, are you?"

Tisdale interrupted, "Don't be daft! Of course he has to tell—"

Before he could finish his sentence, Emma wheeled her horse around. "I knew I couldn't trust either of you," she cried. Throwing a black look at both men, she spurred the animal into action and headed in the direction of the Ashton ranch.

CHAPTER 14

"WE should go after her!" said Tisdale.

"Why?" Birch asked. "What can she do?"

"Well, she could, um," Tisdale sputtered for a moment, then said indignantly, "she ran out on us. Isn't that reason enough to go after her? She might find her brother and warn him about us."

Birch shrugged and replied, "If he's still free, Clem Johnston has more to worry about than you and me."

Tisdale pointed out, "If he's free, we should be looking for Johnston so we can bring him in and collect that reward money. And Miss Johnston might have some useful information for us regarding where her brother might be."

With an almost imperceptible shake of his head, Birch replied, "I think she's told me all she knows." He urged Cactus toward Carson City and said thoughtfully, "Of course, she looked as if she were about to suggest someone who might have had a stronger motive for killing Frank Ashton than her brother, but we were interrupted." He stared meaningfully at Tisdale, but the significance of what he said sailed past his companion.

Although the journey to Carson City was short, they had to pass through Silver City, one of the towns that had sprung up when the Comstock Lode was discovered a few years ago. It was small and dusty and of not much consequence, but their travels were brought to a halt when about ten drunk, brawling men staggered out of a saloon into the middle of the street and held up the flow.

Birch looked around for some way to get around them, but the town was too small for more than one street. He was about to turn his horse around, intending to ride around the outskirts of Silver City, when one of the brawlers tried to pull him down off his horse. Birch kicked the man away.

In the middle of all the confusion, the sound of gunfire sent Tisdale's mount into a restless, skittish dance that took all the authority Tisdale could muster to bring under control.

Birch looked around for the law, then realized that one of the men in the mob scene was wearing a badge. He was the one who'd fired the gun into the air.

Sliding down from Cactus, Birch led his animal to Tisdale, who had, by now, dismounted. Birch handed him the reins to Cactus before wading into the throng. This wasn't a serious fray. This was brawling for the pure enjoyment of it.

Birch approached the lawman carefully, not wanting him to think he was just another brawler. But he needn't have worried because the lawman noticed the ex-Ranger and pulled him off to the side of the street. Up close, Birch realized that the man wasn't wearing a marshal's badge, rather a deputy's.

The deputy spoke wearily. "Something I can do for you, stranger? You don't look like a miner to me."

Birch introduced himself and explained the situation.

The deputy listened carefully, nodding and frowning at all the appropriate places in Birch's story. Then he said, "We had a wire yesterday from the Carson City marshal about that murder. The wanted man was one of Ashton's ranch hands, right?"

"Clem Johnston," Birch stated.

The deputy nodded, clearly recognizing the name. "That's the one."

Birch had to satisfy his curiosity, so he asked, "Do you know anything about Frank Ashton?"

"It was the talk of the town here," the deputy said with relish. "Ashton wasn't a popular man. Or maybe he was, depending on who you ask."

"What do you mean by that?"

With a leer, the deputy replied, "He used to come here on occasion. He liked the women here. We got the prettiest women in the county."

"I see. Anyone in particular?"

"You might ask Lily," the deputy suggested. "She works over at the Desert Flower."

Birch seemed to recall Johnston mentioning Frank Ashton's appetite for women, Silver City being mentioned in particular.

He thanked the lawman and started to walk away. The deputy called after him, "I should have this fracas under control in a few minutes."

Birch doubted that he would, but he knew from experience that fights started out of boredom usually ended soon afterward. The men involved tended to be intoxicated and would either pass out or get knocked out.

Tisdale had taken the horses away from the fray and was waiting very near the Desert Flower Saloon.

"I need to go in there and talk to someone," Birch said.

Tisdale raised his eyebrows. "I thought you wanted to get to Carson City as quickly as possible."

"I do, but there's a woman here who was visited by Frank Ashton quite a lot. I want to ask her a few questions. It shouldn't take more than a few minutes."

It was a small saloon, even by small boomtown standards. But it was decorated with brass fittings, paintings of naked ladies on the walls, and a mirror over the bar. The saloon's opulence advertised that this was a thriving town.

Only two men were present, and they were both unconscious; one was sprawled across a table and the other had slid off his chair onto the floor. No one had bothered to pick him up.

Birch ordered a beer for himself and a whiskey for Tisdale.

"Is Lily around?" he asked the heavyset man behind the bar.

The bartender had muttonchops and a drooping mustache. At the sound of Lily's name, it was all he could do to keep from smirking. "Upstairs and to your right. First door on your left."

Birch left Tisdale to pay for the drinks while he went upstairs and knocked on her door.

He heard a muffled and blurry "Come in" and opened the door carefully.

The room was messy, clothes flung on the chair, the bed, the floor. For a moment, Birch stood in the door, wondering where the owner of the room could be. A mound of clothes on the bed moved and a woman sat up.

A bottle dangled from her right hand over the side of the bed. The woman had deep auburn hair. She was wearing a corset with a filmy robe over it, which revealed much of her plump but attractive figure. She was a handsome woman, if a trifle red-eyed from crying, drinking, or both.

"Lily?" Birch ventured.

"I'm not open for business today, stranger. Take your trade elsewhere." She stood up unsteadily and added, "I'm in mourning."

"For Frank Ashton?"

Lily stumbled toward him. "What do you know about it, mister?" Not waiting for an answer, she continued, "He was going to leave his wife for me, you know. We'd been keeping company for almost a year now. Frank loved me. He was going to take me out of this stinking hole."

Birch had never encountered so much misery with no hope. He was working on a reply when a voice from behind addressed her.

"Miss Lily," the male voice said. Birch turned around and, to his surprise, discovered that it was Tisdale. Tisdale went on, "We're here to ask you a few questions about your friendship with Frank Ashton."

She peered at him blearily. "Why should I answer any of your questions? Frank's dead. Somebody killed him. What good will it do him? It won't bring him back."

"It might bring his killer to justice," Tisdale suggested.

She waved a hand vaguely at them and swayed dangerously to her left. Grabbing hold of the iron bedstead, she righted herself and took a deep breath. "Frank's killer's been caught," Lily slurred. "A young kid. Ranch hand. Just up and stabbed him, from what I heard."

Birch remained silent while Tisdale took control of the conversation. "There's some question as to the young man's guilt. We're looking into it."

With a snort, Lily said, "Far be it from me to stand in the way of justice." She sighed and added, "What do you want to know?"

Tisdale looked at Birch expectantly, waiting for him to ask his questions.

"Did Ashton ever mention the names of his enemies?" Birch asked. "Did any one name come up more often than the others?"

Lily took a swig from an open bottle of rye that sat on a nearby nightstand. After a moment, she said, "He talked about the men who hated him. They were just jealous because he was rich. No one in particular." She blinked and added, "Although . . ."

Birch leaned forward and prompted her. "Although what, Miss Lily?"

She hesitated, shook her head. "I don't think Baker could do such a thing."

"Baker?"

"Bert Baker. Another ranch owner," she explained. "I'm not sure what the problem was between them, but it might have had something to do with Ashton's son. Not the usual feud over land or water or cattle. Frank was very upset the last time I saw him." Her voice broke, whether from emotion or too much liquor, Birch couldn't tell. "It was the only thing he could talk about before passing out on my bed." She took another slug of rye.

Birch thought this over. Bert Baker had not been mentioned by either Clem Johnston or Emma. For that matter, Tisdale hadn't mentioned him either, which meant he wasn't on the Carson City marshal's list of suspects.

With a tip of his hat to the sad woman in the room, Birch left quickly, Tisdale right behind him.

"So who is this Bert Baker?" Tisdale asked.

Birch grimaced. "I thought you could tell me. Did the marshal mention him at all when you talked to him?"

Tisdale shook his head. "What do we do now?"

Birch was still a little disconcerted at having his boss following him around like a puppy. He was grateful that Tisdale had proven himself useful, but Birch felt that the head of Tisdale Investigations had now fallen into the category of millstone.

With a sigh, Birch replied, "We go to Carson City and talk to Clem. And the marshal."

Tisdale nodded solemnly as if that was exactly what he would have suggested. They tossed back their drinks and went back outside.

True to the Silver City deputy's word, the fight had ended, or had scattered to other places. There were a few men lolling on the boardwalk in a state of semiconsciousness and a few more staggering in various directions, probably toward their homes.

Birch and Tisdale mounted their horses and rode out of Silver City at an urgent gallop.

CHAPTER 15

CARSON City was the largest town in southern Nevada Territory. People in fashionable city clothes walked down the main street at a brisk pace. Stagecoaches rattled down the thoroughfare toward their various destinations. Horse-and-buggies clip-clopped along at a slower gait. A stranger entering Carson City for the first time might want to slow down and take it all in.

However, Birch and Tisdale wasted no time. They searched for and found the jail. It was a wide, squat wooden building with a discreet sign above the front door that read "Carson City County Jail." Even if the sign hadn't been there, Birch wouldn't have had to be much of a detective to find it—it was, after all, the only building on the main street with bars on the windows.

Dismounting, they left the horses tied to a hitching post thoughtfully provided outside the jail. Inside, the marshal's office was more civilized than most of the frontier town jails that Birch had visited. Visitors came up against a low fence-like barrier when entering the Carson City County Jail. Beyond the barricade was a large oak desk to the right of the front door and flanking it were two other smaller wooden desks.

There was one man occupying one of the lesser desks and he looked up at Birch and Tisdale's entrance. He was young, with a pimply face and wire-rim bifocals. In his blue pin-stripe shirt and dark gray flannel pants and matching vest, he looked more like a clerk than a lawman. The only way Birch could tell he was a deputy was by the tin star modestly displayed on his vest.

Squinting, the deputy put his pencil down and stood up. "Can I help you gentlemen?"

Birch felt like he was in church, so with an uncharacteristic gesture he took off his hat. He was dusty from his ride and out of place in this fancy city jailhouse. He decided to try the direct approach. "We understand that you have Clem Johnston locked up."

The deputy fixed the two strangers with a sharp look and cautiously replied, "We might. Why do you ask?"

Birch explained who he was and why he was here. The deputy's expression went from suspicious to amused. He took his wire frames off and wiped them with his white linen handkerchief before asking, "So what do you want from us? The reward? You let him escape and we caught him right here in Carson City. I'm not authorized to reward incompetence."

His jaw set, Birch fought the feeling of dislike that was welling up inside him. Through gritted teeth, he asked, "Is the marshal around? We have some business to discuss."

"No, he's not here right now" was the curt reply.

Birch tried again. "Well, can we see Clem Johnston? I'd like to talk to him for a few minutes."

The deputy had gone back to his desk and pulled a sheaf of papers out of a drawer. He was going over them intently as if ignoring Birch and Tisdale would make them give up and go away.

He finally looked up and said, "Oh. You're still here?"

Birch had had enough. He vaulted over the low barrier and strode over to the deputy. The young man's face paled. He had to pull back in his chair to look up at the tall agent.

"I'd like to talk with Clem Johnston," Birch said in a low voice that held the hint of a threat as he loomed over the rude deputy. "If you can't help me, tell me where I can find the marshal and I'll tell him all about our conversation."

The deputy's hands trembled as he replied in a shaky voice, "You'll have to leave your gun with me." His eyes left

Birch's face long enough to watch him withdraw his gun
from its holster and place it on the desk between them. His
eyes fastened to Birch's impassive face, the young man slowly
stood up.

"You should have another gun and a rifle of mine here,"
Birch admitted, straightening up. "Johnston would have had
a Navy Colt in his possession, along with a Colt repeater rifle,
when he was captured."

The deputy threw Birch a curious look, but looked away
quickly, his shaky fingers trying to find the right key to the
jail cell.

Tisdale came over. "I'm not carrying a gun," he told the
deputy, then turned to Birch. "What exactly do you want to
talk to him about, Birch?"

Birch shook his head. "What you and I discussed back in
Hazen. And I'm going to let him know that Emma is back in
town. I'll make it quick. If you want to make any money out
of this situation, Mr. Tisdale, I suggest that you allow me to
help young Johnston in there by finding Ashton's real
murderer."

Tisdale nodded. The deputy led them toward a door in
the back wall. He paused after opening it and said to Tisdale,
"I'm sorry, sir. Only one visitor at a time." Having caught
Birch's dark look, he swallowed hard, drew himself up, and
added, "It's policy."

Birch raised his eyebrows at Tisdale. The retired colonel
bowed and stepped back, saying, "We certainly can't go
against policy now, can we?"

The deputy looked relieved. Birch followed him through
the door.

Although it wasn't apparent from the main street, Carson
City County Jail was a fairly large building. The jail contained
ten cells and many of them were occupied by an assortment
of grimy and shifty characters. Clem Johnston had been
installed in a cell at the far end of the corridor.

It had only been a few days since Birch had last seen him,

but inside the cell, Johnston looked older, more careworn. When the accused killer looked up at the approaching men, Birch noted that his eyes didn't have the fire in them that they used to have. Clem Johnston looked as though he'd lost all hope.

At the sight of Birch, a spark of interest perked the prisoner up. He grabbed the cell bars and leaned forward. A moment later, maybe having thought twice about it, Johnston slumped back onto his cot. Maybe he was weary of having his hopes dashed.

The deputy pulled a rickety stool from against the back wall and set it down outside the cell.

"Five minutes" was all he said before leaving.

"Johnston, I've come here to help you."

Johnston stared at the ceiling, ignoring Birch. A few other prisoners called out to him.

"He don't want no help, stranger," one prisoner said. "He just lays there all day long, not saying anything."

Another man replied, "Yeah, why don't you help someone around here who wants help. Like me. I could use it. I didn't do it."

Laughter filled the cold hallway.

Birch ignored them and tried again. "What made you come back?"

Johnston sighed and sat up. "Why did you bother to come here? No one can help me now. I walked right into a trap." He got up from his cot and started pacing. "Emma was right. I should have run when I had the chance. But I thought I could prove I didn't kill Mr. Ashton."

"How did you think you could prove that?"

Johnston stopped and stared thoughtfully at Birch. Finally, he said, "I thought I could find the owner of the knife."

"Did you?"

Johnston shook his head.

Birch tried again. "Where were you arrested?"

"At the Double B Ranch south of Carson City. Mr. Baker owns it."

"Why did you go there?" Birch wanted to know.

"Because that's the place I remember seeing the knife." Johnston paused, then explained, "The Bakers had a barn raising a few months ago, and right after that, they gave a party. The surrounding ranch owners and their hands all had a part in helping the Bakers build it and I guess the dance was their way of thanking their neighbors for their help."

Birch nodded to show that he understood, but stayed silent, letting Johnston continue. "Well, I had a lot to drink that night. Later, I remember someone showing me the knife, but I can't recall who. I thought maybe Bert Baker could help me out."

Birch asked, "How did you recognize the knife in the first place? What makes it so special? And why did you think Baker would help you, knowing that you were wanted for killing Ashton?"

Clem Johnston looked sheepish and answered the last question first. "Well, Mr. Baker is a nice fellow. I guess I thought he'd listen to me before turning me over to the law."

"But Baker turned you over to the marshal?" Birch asked.

Johnston shook his head. "No, I never got to see Baker. It turned out that he was away from the ranch. One of his ranch hands recognized me and sent for the marshal. As for the knife, well, I told you before that it wasn't an ordinary one. It has this carved handle made of ivory or bone with a long, curved blade. A nasty-looking blade."

Birch listened thoughtfully and said, "In other words, not a knife that a ranch hand might carry around."

The boy's face brightened. "Hey, that's right . . ." His face fell again. "But they'd just say I stole it."

Birch reminded him, "But the owner of the knife hasn't come forward yet. That might mean something."

Johnston leaned forward eagerly. "Is there a chance for me?"

Pausing for only a heartbeat, Birch said, "A chance."

"I'm sorry I caused all that trouble for you, Mr. Birch." Birch had to suppress a smile. Johnston looked younger, almost boyish, now. "I hope you don't hold it against me or Emma for pulling that trick on you. I don't suppose you know it yet, but Emma's my sister. I hope she's all right. I left her back in Hazen in that boardinghouse. Didn't want her to get into any trouble with the law back here."

"I'm afraid she didn't stay there. She came back here with us," Birch informed the young prisoner.

Clem Johnston looked surprised. "She did? Is she with you out in the marshal's office? I'd sure like to see her."

"She left us at the crossroads, so to speak. We had a disagreement. She wanted to go toward the Ashton ranch, and Tisdale and I wanted to come here first."

Clem Johnston seemed to tense up, his fingers gripping the bars of his cell until his knuckles whitened. He started rocking himself back and forth, almost unconsciously, and solemnly said, "Mr. Birch, I don't ask much of you. You don't need to find the killer, but I'd appreciate it if you'd look out for my sister for me. I know her well and if she followed me here against my wishes and finds out I'm in jail, she might go poking around and get herself into trouble. I don't think I could live with myself knowing Emma came to a terrible end on my account."

Birch heard the jail door opening at the end of the corridor and realized that the interview was coming to an end.

From the short time that he had known Emma, Birch had learned that she was bright, resourceful, and loved her brother very much. He thought it was extremely likely that she might start asking questions that would get her killed.

With this thought foremost in his mind, Birch stood up.

"I'll start looking for her, Clem. Chances are that she went back to the Ashton ranch. It's only been a few hours since we parted ways. How much trouble can she get in?"

She can get herself killed, Birch thought, but he didn't bother to answer his own question aloud.

With Clem Johnston's thanks ringing in his ears, Birch was escorted out of the jail by the deputy.

CHAPTER 16

TISDALE was sitting down when Birch walked back into the marshal's office. The marshal walked through the front door a moment later. Tisdale stood up and moved over to Birch's side.

"Marshal Turner," the young deputy said. "I'm glad you're back. Maybe you can clear this up." He gestured with annoyance toward Birch and Tisdale.

The marshal nodded curtly to his subordinate and turned to study the two men. Tisdale took the opportunity to size up the lawman as well. Turner reminded him of a younger Jefferson Birch; he was tall and thin and was in his late twenties. He had a long clean-shaven face, but that was where his resemblance to Birch ended. When he took his hat off, Marshal Turner revealed a prominent forehead with thinning sandy hair combed straight back. More casually dressed than his assistant, he wore a pair of denims that had seen better days, a faded red cotton shirt with a black string tie, and a worn black vest. His boots were scuffed and scratched as well.

Ignoring the lawman, Tisdale turned to Birch and asked, "What did you find out?" He was anxious to find out if Clem Johnston had given important information to Birch.

Before Birch could reply, the marshal surveyed the situation and asked the deputy, "What's going on here, Fred?"

The deputy pushed Tisdale aside and, in a whiny voice, said, "Marshal Turner, these men walked in here and threatened me. The big one," he indicated Birch, "bullied me into taking him back to the cells so he could talk to one of the prisoners."

100

Turner turned a baleful eye upon his underling and asked, "Which prisoner?"

Birch answered, "Clem Johnston."

The marshal's face softened slightly. He said, "That's Emma Johnston's brother, the boy who's accused of killing Frank Ashton, right?"

Humiliated by the marshal's indifference, the deputy turned back to the paperwork on his desk.

The three men sat down, Marshal Turner behind his oak desk, Birch and Tisdale facing him in two chairs.

"Now, what's this all about?" Turner asked when they'd finally gotten settled.

Tisdale waited for Birch to launch into an explanation, but was surprised when his companion passed a hand over his face, a gesture of quiet exasperation.

"I think I'll let Mr. Tisdale tell you," Birch said.

Tisdale was pleased. This was the first time Birch had shown such deference and it made him feel accepted by his agent. He briefly wondered if Birch was really tired, or if he'd just decided that his employer's explanation might carry more weight. Either way, Arthur Tisdale puffed himself up to his full height, trying to give an impression of a cross between dignity and humility. With that, he introduced himself and Birch, then launched into an account of their experiences of the past several days.

When he got to Johnston's escape, he skipped a good bit of the detail to save them both embarrassment, but other than that, the account was complete and concise. The important fact was that Johnston was back in custody and he made sure he gave the marshal full credit for that.

When he was finished, Marshal Turner wore an amused smile. He leaned back in his chair, pressing his fingertips together over his chest.

"So that's where Emma Johnston went," Turner said thoughtfully. "We were looking for her, of course."

Tisdale hurriedly added, "Of course, you can't really

blame her, Marshal. After all, he is her brother. I hope you won't punish her too harshly for aiding the escape of a killer."

"Accused killer," Turner reminded him. "And no, I wasn't planning on throwing Miss Johnston in the pokey for acting as any close relative would under the circumstances."

Tisdale was surprised at how lax the county marshal was being, but he supposed this was another example of frontier justice at work.

He ventured one more question. "Then you won't be locking her up?"

"Nope." Turner made a dismissive gesture with one hand, then soberly added, "But I'll have a little talk with her sometime about obstructing the law and abetting a wanted man."

There was a softness to the marshal's voice when he said Emma Johnston's name. Tisdale wondered if he was sweet on her.

Birch spoke up. "Marshal, it appears to me that you're a man who believes Clem Johnston might be innocent."

Marshal Turner hesitated, then said, "Let's just say that I believe in a man's innocence until he's found guilty in a court of law."

Birch countered with, "But would you say that he had a good motive for killing Frank Ashton?"

Marshal Turner blinked. "Mr. Birch and Mr. Tisdale, what is your interest in all this? It seems to me that you lost your bounty, and the reward that goes with it, a few days ago. Johnston is locked up. Why are you still interested?"

It was a good question. The past few days, Tisdale had wondered why he was still here. It was Birch who fiercely believed in Clem Johnston's innocence. Off and on, Tisdale had thought about catching the next stagecoach back to San Francisco. The reason for his presence had been to watch how Birch handled himself when he was working for Tisdale Investigations. That had ended when Johnston escaped.

While Tisdale didn't blame Birch for the disappointing results—sometimes he still blamed himself for being in Birch's way—he often felt it would be prudent for him to leave. Nevertheless, he stayed on, his curiosity getting the better of him—what would Jefferson Birch do next?

"When I got a wire from Mr. Tisdale here," Birch explained, "I spent a few days hunting down Clem Johnston up in northern Nevada Territory. I found him in Pine Ridge and trailed him about ten miles before finally capturing him."

Birch hesitated, then went on in the same unhurried manner. "I had a few days to get to know him. I used to be a Ranger back in Texas, so I've been at this sort of job for a few years now, and when I get a feeling that a man's innocent, I can't just walk away from it. Even if there's no money involved." He leaned forward to make his point. "This is about a man's life."

Turner nodded, a pensive look on his face. "I believe you, Birch. Tell me, what can I do for you?"

"I need information about the circumstances of Frank Ashton's death."

The marshal said amiably, "Go on, ask your questions. I'll answer them to the best of my ability."

Birch continued, "Johnston mentioned that the knife was unusual."

"That's so." Turner leaned over and unlocked his bottom drawer. "I have it right here." He pulled it out and placed it on his desk.

There had been a halfhearted attempt to wipe the dagger, but it was still dulled by old blood. The blade was about nine or ten inches long and curved. Tisdale shuddered at the thought of such an evil-looking blade killing someone. The handle was ivory and carved with strange symbols that reminded Tisdale of far-off exotic lands.

Birch picked it up and studied it silently, then passed it on to Tisdale without comment. Tisdale scrutinized it for a moment, careful not to touch the bloody blade, then set it back down on the desktop.

"Not the usual sort of knife you can buy at any good supply store or smithy" was Birch's dry comment.

Marshal Turner's face remained impassive, but his eyes locked with Birch's eyes for a moment and Tisdale sensed that he was in agreement.

"You must have seen the body," Birch said. "And you must have seen Johnston."

Marshal Turner looked distinctly uncomfortable. He rubbed the back of his neck and exhaled loudly. "I really didn't get a close look at the body, but it wasn't a pretty sight. Johnston was being held at gunpoint by John Ashton."

Birch nodded. "What about Johnston's clothes? You saw him before he escaped. Was there any blood on his shirt?"

Turner looked thoughtful. "Now there again, you have me at a disadvantage. When I came into the barn, it was so dark. The only thing I can positively say is that Johnston was wearing a dark-colored shirt." He shifted uncomfortably in his seat as he recalled, "I'm embarrassed to admit this, but Clem Johnston got the gun away from John Ashton almost the minute I walked in there. Staring down the barrel of a gun didn't give me an awful lot of time to notice something like that. Maybe Frank's widow and son would know. They spent more time with him, waiting for my arrival. The doctor came with me also. Maybe he was more observant than me."

"Do you know of anyone around here," Birch asked, "who might have had reason to kill Frank Ashton?"

The marshal's face twitched slightly and he looked away. "I'm sure you've asked that question before, Birch. What was the answer?"

Birch sighed. "Just about everyone had a reason to kill Frank Ashton. Both Clem Johnston and his sister told me that. I was hoping you might be able to narrow down the list of suspects."

"If I'd been able to do that, Clem Johnston might not be

in jail." Turner stood up and stretched. "Can't think of anyone with enough reason to kill the man though. Frank Ashton was a lying, cheating son of a bitch who thought everyone was out to get him. And with good reason. I guess it just took the right man with the wrong nature to pick up a knife and murder him. Even his own family hated him. Ashton ruled his son's life with an iron fist. The boy couldn't make a decision on his own, the way Ashton brought him up. I don't know what's going to happen to the ranch with just the widow and son running it now."

Tisdale decided it was time to jump in with a question of his own. "Marshal Turner, do you know of anyone who has a collection of knives? Someone who was perhaps acquainted with Frank Ashton?"

The marshal frowned and slowly shook his head. Tisdale tried again. "Perhaps this someone doesn't collect just knives," he suggested. "Maybe this person has a collection of things from his travels to exotic places."

Turner raised his eyebrows, an idea forming on his face. "Yes, there is someone like that. Bert Baker of the Double B Ranch."

Tisdale remembered hearing the name. He saw Birch flinch in recognition. Had Emma mentioned it?

He asked, "And where is the Baker ranch?"

"Why, just a few miles east of the Ashton place," the marshal replied, then added, "but Bert Baker couldn't have killed Ashton. He's been away since before the killing. He just got back a fortnight ago."

Birch said, "But someone was around the Baker ranch during the Ashton killing, right?"

"Sure, there were some ranch hands and the foreman."

Birch and Tisdale stood up.

"Thank you for your time, Marshal," Tisdale said gratefully. "You've been a big help."

Marshal Turner said, "You might want to talk to that doctor

I told you about. He hangs his shingle just down the street from here. His name's Wheeler."

Birch thanked him again, they all shook hands, then the two men turned to leave.

Birch seemed to remember something and turned back around. "By the way, Marshal, you wouldn't happen to have a Navy Colt and a Sharps carbine in your gun collection, would you?"

Marshal Turner broke into a wide grin and said, "I believe I do." He opened the bottom drawer of his desk and rummaged around.

"Just happen to have one in here." The lawman pulled out Birch's Navy Colt, checked the chambers, and tossed it to him.

Birch caught it and hefted it. "Feels about right."

Marshal Turner then went to his rifle rack, pulled down a carbine, and asked, "This the one?"

Birch nodded and took it, checking the cylinder.

After they left the jailhouse, Birch tucked the carbine under his arm, drew the Smith & Wesson out of his holster, and slid the Navy Colt in. He gave Tisdale the other gun, saying, "We'll have to get you a holster later."

Tisdale took it and handled it gingerly for a moment. "Thank you, Birch," he said as he stuck it in his belt.

Birch grinned and said, "You paid for it."

Doc Wheeler's wife answered the door. She was a plump and pleasant-looking woman but Birch could tell that she was hesitant about letting them in, but he certainly didn't blame her for her concern. Here were two strangers, one with a gun tucked in his waistband, the other armed with a gun in his holster and a rifle hanging from one hand. But she reluctantly admitted them.

"My husband is with a patient right now, but if you can wait, he shouldn't be much longer." She looked at Tisdale's bandaged shoulder and quickly left.

A piercing yell came from the other side of a door marked

"Surgery." Birch and Tisdale exchanged dubious glances. Another scream filled the office. Tisdale shifted nervously in his seat.

Birch reminded him, "Don't worry. I won't let the good doctor touch you, Mr. Tisdale."

They both chuckled.

The surgery door opened and an elderly man limped out with the help of a crutch, followed by a middle-aged man who was wiping his hands with a towel.

"Thank ye, Doc," the patient said. "How much do I owe ye fer yer trouble?"

Doctor Wheeler indicated his wife, who had come into the room unobtrusively, and said, "Mrs. Wheeler will figure out what you owe. And next time you're cleaning your Spencer rifle, Henry," he warned, "don't put it down on your chair when you get distracted by something else. Those rifles are temperamental. You'll have some trouble sitting for a while, but use a pillow. Be thankful your injuries weren't worse."

Henry grimaced and nodded. Doctor Wheeler turned his attention to Birch and Tisdale.

He asked, "Which one of you is next?"

Tisdale jumped. Birch smiled and said, "We're here on a matter that isn't entirely medical. My name is Jefferson Birch and this is Mr. Arthur Tisdale." He explained the purpose of their visit.

"I see," the doctor said, looking at Tisdale's shoulder. "Why don't we step into my surgery? I can look at that wound while we're discussing the Ashton killing."

The surgery had the smell of borax and lye soap. Two chairs were lined up against one wall, a table against another wall held different surgical instruments, and a high narrow examination table sat in the middle of the room. A medicine cabinet was built on the wall above the surgical instrument table. A sink sat in a corner of the room and it was here that Doctor Wheeler strode over to a large ceramic bowl and pitcher. He poured out fresh water and washed up before examining his new patient.

He indicated the examination table to Tisdale, who sat gingerly on the edge of it. Birch took a seat and watched with amusement.

"Now then," Wheeler said as he dried his hands with a clean towel, "what do you want to know?"

Tisdale was too nervous to talk, so Birch began. "Did you examine the body at the Ashton place or back here in your office?"

The doctor had taken the bandage off of Tisdale's shoulder and was peering at the healing wound. "Um hm. We brought the body back here."

"Was there a lot of blood?"

The doctor probed his patient's shoulder. Tisdale jumped a bit. "Ouch!"

The doctor looked over at his patient and said, "You're lucky you came to me today. Your wound is infected. I'll have to clean it out a bit with alcohol." He reached over for a bottle of rubbing alcohol and another clean rag. "Now this is going to sting some. Try not to move around too much."

He began daubing alcohol on Tisdale's shoulder and said to Birch, "I'm sorry. You wanted to know if there was much blood? Well, of course there was. If you were stabbed with a vicious-looking blade like the one young Johnston was holding, you'd be bleeding like a stuck pig, too. I trust the marshal showed you the murder weapon?"

"Yes," Birch confirmed. "But I just wanted to confirm that so I could ask my next question."

"Which is?" the doctor asked as he efficiently bound a long cloth strip around the wounded shoulder.

"Wouldn't the blood get on the killer's clothes as well? Did you happen to notice Johnston's shirt?"

Doctor Wheeler stopped bandaging for a moment. He looked thoughtfully at Tisdale, then at Birch. "That's a very good question. You're right, of course. The killer would be bound to have blood on whatever he was wearing. You know, I can't say for sure if Johnston had any blood on him. I'm sure you know the effects on a person's eyes when they go from bright sun to near darkness. Both the marshal and I did just such a thing. I think Johnston realized that it was a perfect opportunity to escape. Probably the only chance he would ever get.

"So when we came into the barn, and Mrs. Ashton stumbled into her son, who was holding a gun on Johnston, the boy took advantage of everyone's confusion, tackled John Ashton, and got the gun. He ordered everyone to drop their weapons into a nearby haystack, then took the only saddled horse in the stable, and left."

Tisdale asked, "What about your horse and the marshal's horse—weren't they left outside the barn?"

The doctor chuckled. "Not when we finally got out there. Johnston had taken them away, leaving them in a pasture on the far side of the Ashton property. By the time we got the horses and our weapons, the only thing the marshal could do was go back to Carson City and call up a posse. Didn't do much good. Very few men volunteered. Frank Ashton was not well liked and I'm afraid more than a few people are glad that he's dead."

Tisdale slipped his shirt back on and buttoned it.

Birch stood up and said, "Well, thank you for your time, Doctor."

The physician waved his hand. "Not at all. Glad to help. Thing is, I like Clem Johnston. Most people around here do, too. I wish I had paid a little more attention to young Johnston's shirt. I know it doesn't help you any."

Birch tried once more. "Was there anything unusual about the killing?"

The doctor's face became grim. "I can tell you this much—whoever killed Frank Ashton hated him. He'd been stabbed more than once."

Birch asked, "How many times?"

The doctor went over to his desk and glanced at a paper. "Six times."

Tisdale spoke up. "I was wondering, Doctor. Have you ever been out to Bert Baker's ranch? Maybe you've seen his collection."

The doctor's face brightened. "Ah, yes. He has an interesting accumulation of weapons and miscellany from Africa and India, where he was stationed. He was a commissioned officer in the British Army for many years."

Tisdale dug into his pocket, obviously intending to pay for the medical attention. Doctor Wheeler showed them out of the office and said to his waiting wife, "Don't charge them anything, Frances. They came in to talk about the Johnston boy."

Birch and Tisdale thanked them both and headed for the Baker ranch.

CHAPTER 17

THE Double B Ranch was about ten miles southeast from Carson City. The road wound through mountain passes and valleys until Birch and Tisdale came up against a fence with a sign proclaiming the land beyond to be the property of the Double B. They followed the fence until they came to a well-traveled path that led to the main house.

Chickens scattered out of Cactus's way, pigs routed in the mud of a sty built onto the side of the barn, and cows grazed in the pasture beyond. Between the main house and the barn was a simple bunkhouse, which looked to be empty. Three unsaddled horses were tethered to a hitching post near the barn; one of them looked like the horse Emma had been riding.

Birch reined Cactus in warily. He put a hand out and gestured for Tisdale to stay quiet as well. Slowly, he unfastened the tie on his holster.

As Birch eased out of the saddle, the front door to the main house opened and a woman stepped out. She was older, maybe in her fifties, and wore her graying hair swept up. An apron covered most of her light-colored calico dress. Her sleeves were rolled up, her bare arms dusted with flour as if she'd been making bread. Her face was open and friendly.

"What can I do for you, strangers?" she asked in a pleasant English accent. Then she frowned, adding in a tone filled with regret, "If you're looking for ranch work, I'm afraid we're all filled up. But I can give you a meal."

Birch instantly liked her and, after glancing at Tisdale, noted that he, too, was charmed enough to doff his hat.

"Thank you, ma'am." Birch tipped his hat to her, then

walked to the main house's hitching post to tether Cactus, and continued, "My name is Jefferson Birch and this is Arthur Tisdale."

"I'm Irene Baker."

"Mrs. Baker," Birch began. "We're looking into Frank Ashton's murder."

She wiped her hands on her apron and said, "I was in San Francisco at the time." On a grim note, Mrs. Baker added, "And even if I'd witnessed the Johnston boy do it, I certainly wouldn't be the one to send him to the gallows."

Birch raised his eyebrows. "Then you think Clem Johnston did it?"

Irene Baker looked pensive as she replied, "No, it doesn't seem likely to me. I've known Clem and his sister Emma for a long time and"—she shook her head—"I just can't picture it."

"What I was wondering about was your husband's collection. Is he around?"

Irene Baker's eyes stared beyond Birch's shoulder. "A moment ago, I would have said no, but he's just riding up now."

Birch and Tisdale turned around. An impressive man sat astride a large red roan. He was in his late fifties, hale and hearty, with a military bearing and a neat gray mustache. Several ranch hands rode up with him and it was apparent that they'd spent the day out on the range, hard at work. Baker rode up to his wife, jumped off his roan and pulled her to him.

"You've been baking bread again, haven't you, Irene? I hope it's your soda bread," he said in a clipped British accent. "You know how much the boys like it!"

He broke away and tethered the handsome roan, glancing at Birch and Tisdale.

Birch stood by impatiently, certain Baker had been aware of them since riding up to the main house.

He finally turned to Birch and Tisdale and asked his wife, "Won't you introduce me to these two gentlemen, Irene?"

Mrs. Baker stepped forward and replied, "Bert, Mr. Birch and Mr. Tisdale are interested in the Ashton murder. Mr. Birch was just asking me about your collection."

Baker nodded gravely. "That was a bad thing, that killing. Not that Frank Ashton didn't deserve a good pounding, mind you." He sized up the two men and said, "What do you want to know?"

Tisdale answered him. "The knife that Clem Johnston was found holding was of Indian origin, I believe. Carved ivory handle with a wicked-looking curved blade, about nine inches long."

Pushing his hat back a fraction, Baker looked troubled. "The wife and I were in San Francisco on business. Until today I just assumed it was an ordinary knife, a Bowie or something similar. But it sounds like one I used to have. It has a carved ivory sheath as well."

Birch asked, "Used to have?"

Bert Baker nodded. "It was stolen a few months ago. I've always suspected that the Ashton boy took it. Every time he was over here, I'd find him standing in front of it, admiring the handle. But he's such a troubled lad that I didn't dare accuse him of such a thing for fear his father would hear of it. His father treated him worse than he would treat a dog."

Mrs. Baker nodded solemnly and added, "John Ashton is a strange one."

Birch's first impulse was to jump on Cactus and ride hellbent toward the Ashton ranch, but he stayed calm. The pieces were beginning to fit into place. Several people had mentioned that Frank Ashton controlled his son's life. It had also been mentioned more than once that John Ashton was troubled or strange.

Possible scenes flashed through Birch's mind: maybe John had been pushed too far that day in an argument with his father. Maybe the argument was over the knife. Maybe Frank

Ashton discovered that his son had possession of it and recognized it as being from Mr. Baker's collection. Maybe John Ashton lost control and lashed out with the stolen weapon. It would be a fitting, if not an ugly, end for Frank Ashton.

If John had killed his father, how had he gotten out of the barn without Clem Johnston seeing him? Birch would have to have a look at the barn. No doubt it would be easy enough to slip out of a side door unseen. Once he was out, John could have changed clothes and cleaned himself up so no one would suspect that he was his father's killer.

Shaking off his preoccupation, Birch asked, "Mr. and Mrs. Baker, I noticed that Emma Johnston's horse is tethered out by your barn. Is she here? Can I speak to her?"

Mrs. Baker wrinkled her forehead, betraying her dismay. "Oh, I'm afraid she's gone. She came in here a little over an hour ago and I made her something to eat before she rode off. Her horse had ridden long and hard, and needed a rest, so I let her borrow one of ours."

"I saw her just about half an hour ago," Mr. Baker added. "I was just about to tell you that I ran into her. She asked me about my knife, too. Then she was heading for the Ashton ranch." He got a worried look on his face. "I hope she's not going to do anything foolish."

Birch's stomach tightened. He looked at Tisdale. Tisdale looked at Birch. And it appeared that they were thinking the same thing.

CHAPTER 18

MARTHA Ashton opened the door to Emma's knock. Her reaction was much better than what Emma had expected. Mrs. Ashton looked momentarily disconcerted. "What are you doing here, Emma?"

"Mrs. Ashton," Emma rushed her words, hoping to get them out before the widow closed her door. "I think we need to talk. It's about Clem."

Emma couldn't be sure, but she thought she detected relief in Mrs. Ashton's eyes. After a moment, the widow stepped back and allowed Emma to pass through.

Martha Ashton was wearing black silk. The fabric rustled quietly as she moved ahead of Emma, heading into the parlor.

When they were seated, Mrs. Ashton remained quiet, waiting to hear what Emma had come to say.

"I'm sorry for what happened to your husband, Mrs. Ashton."

In an almost kind voice, Mrs. Ashton replied, "I appreciate your condolences, Emma. We all know what my husband was like—not too many people grieved his passing."

A pained expression came to her face, then Martha Ashton politely asked, "Would you like some tea? I have some water heating up in the kitchen."

Emma felt guilty about her ulterior motive for being there. She sensed that the Ashton widow was lonely and would like to talk to someone—but not the sister of the accused killer. Pushing the guilt away, Emma accepted her offer of tea. Martha Ashton's face relaxed and she excused herself to get it, leaving Emma alone in the parlor.

She sat still for a heartbeat, just in case someone came in unexpectedly, then got up and methodically searched the room for the ivory sheath that Bert Baker had described to her.

Emma had been in the Ashton house many times before, and most of the rooms were decorated with a masculine hand. But the parlor had a mahogany settee upholstered in rich blue with a matching chair, an Oriental rug done in blues and reds, mahogany tables with intricately carved legs, and a magnificent mantelpiece surrounding the fireplace.

However, right now she was looking for something—maybe the sheath that Mr. Baker mentioned, maybe a bloodied shirt. Anything that would set her brother free, and convict the real killer. She started with the cushions of the sofa. Maybe evidence could be hidden there.

Emma opened a carved cherrywood box on top of the writing desk by the window. There was nothing in it but sealing wax with the accompanying stamp, and a bottle of India ink. The drawers on either side of the desk held only sheaves of paper, pens, and several letters that were apparently from Martha Ashton's sister. Emma put everything back the way she'd found it.

She crossed the room and opened the drawers in several small tables. Nothing. Another box stood on the mantel, but it was empty—only a decoration. Standing in the center of the room, Emma took stock of her situation and came to the conclusion that there was nowhere else in this room to hide anything.

Emma wondered how she'd gotten such a crazy notion in the first place. *Pure desperation,* she thought. She couldn't inspect every room in the Ashton house in such a covert manner. Her heart sank.

And what if there wasn't any evidence hidden in the house? The Ashtons owned acres of land. An ivory sheath could have been thrown into a stream or just hurled into woods. It could remain lost for years. A shirt could have been burned.

She would need proof to convince anyone else that John had killed his father. The Ashtons were powerful ranch owners in this county. Even if Bert Baker tells the marshal that he believes John stole the knife, it might be too late to save Clem. By that time, he'd have been hanged for another man's crime. Besides, it would be John's word against Bert's.

Emma barely caught the faint sound of rustling silk approaching. She slipped back onto the sofa as if she'd been waiting there patiently all along.

Martha Ashton entered with a beautiful silver service and two paper-thin bone china cups and saucers. As Martha Ashton poured the tea, Emma thought back to the time when Frank Ashton was still alive. He'd treated his wife like a servant, and there were rumors that he kept a mistress in Silver City. Emma had also heard that Frank Ashton had women he visited when he went on the cattle drives in the fall and the spring.

At the Bakers' barn dance a few months ago, a drunk Frank Ashton had followed Emma around, waiting to get her alone. She shuddered as she remembered his rough hands grabbing her arms, his sour breath, and the spittle she'd seen on his mustache when he pushed his face up close to hers.

"C'mon, Emma," Frank Ashton had slurred. "Let's go some place where we can be 'lone. You're too good fer these other fellas . . . I c'n set you up with a little place of your own and come visit you when I feel like it."

Emma didn't even dignify his lewd proposal with an answer. She twisted in his grip, but Frank Ashton was too strong for her. While he tried to kiss her, Clem spotted them and strode over. He pulled his drunk boss off her, and was about to give him a sound thrashing when a couple of ranch hands pulled him away from Ashton.

Later Clem told Emma that he'd almost lost his job as a result. But Mrs. Ashton had witnessed the incident and the next morning Ashton had grudgingly told Clem he could keep his job.

"Just stay out of my way next time," he growled.

Clem laughed as he recounted his response. "I told him, 'You stay away from my sister, damn it!' "

Martha Ashton was watching Emma warily, the silver creamer in her hand poised over Emma's teacup. "Would you like sugar and cream?"

Emma blinked. "Uh, yes. Just a touch of cream."

Mrs. Ashton handed her the fragile china cup, then stirred cream and sugar into her own cup.

"Why did you really come to see me, Emma?" Her voice was brittle. Her face had hardened. Apparently, she didn't want to keep up this pretense any longer.

Emma was stymied by the question. "Why? . . . well," she stammered, "I just thought . . . that you might like some company." She looked away and added, "We're both suffering from personal losses and . . ."

Mrs. Ashton cocked her head. Her voice was softer this time. "You don't think your brother is guilty, do you, Emma?"

Emma sighed. To all the world, Martha Ashton appeared to be Frank's mousy little wife, but at times she displayed a surprising amount of backbone.

"No, I don't think he's guilty."

Mrs. Ashton sipped her tea. "That's good. Family should stay together, no matter what the circumstances."

On impulse, Emma asked, "What about you, Mrs. Ashton? Do you think my brother is guilty?"

The question appeared to upset Mrs. Ashton. She suddenly became remote, avoiding Emma's direct gaze and putting her teacup down with a clatter. "I wish I could doubt his guilt, but I went into the barn less than a minute after it happened. I saw Clem standing over my husband's body with the knife in his hand."

"Then why in heaven's name did you ask me such a question?"

Martha Ashton did not reply. She looked straight at Emma and in that moment, Emma was struck by the terrible truth that Frank Ashton's widow had to live with: she knew that John had killed his father. But she would never speak up about it.

The widow stiffened and became remote. She said evasively, "I just think it's important for a family to stay close and never doubt each other."

On impulse, Emma touched Mrs. Ashton's hand, feeling her pain. She said, "Mrs. Ashton, I know Clem isn't guilty. And so do you. I came here looking for proof. But I didn't get it." She looked toward the parlor door and said, "I think I'd better go now."

Mrs. Ashton's head was bent and she didn't say anything for a long time. Emma began to wonder if she should just get up and leave. Finally, the widow heaved a sigh and said, "Please follow me."

Emma nodded, at a loss for words. She got up and let Mrs. Ashton lead her out of the parlor and down the hall to a set of closed doors. Emma wondered why they were entering the library. From her dress pocket, the widow took a set of keys and fitted one into the lock.

Mrs. Ashton remained silent, not looking at Emma. It was almost as if Emma were a ghost to her. The library doors opened and Mrs. Ashton stepped in, gliding across the room to the safe in the corner.

Could it be that in her own way she was trying to help Clem—at the expense of her own son? Emma felt a cold shiver run down her spine as she remembered the look of torment in the widow's eyes when she talked about never doubting your family. She was talking about her son, John.

Emma remembered the few times she'd been in his presence. There was something infinitely sad about him, but when he turned his eyes on her, she remembered the prickly sensation on the back of her neck and the feeling that would come over her that she absolutely must get away from John.

The library had the stale smell of pipe smoke. The room must have been closed up since Frank Ashton's death. Heavy brown curtains kept most of the sun out, although a ray had slipped between a crack giving the room a dim dusty light, enough light for Emma to watch Mrs. Ashton bend toward the safe's dial and deftly twirl the combination.

A moment later, the safe's door was open. Instead of taking anything out, the widow stood up and, without looking at Emma, glided past her as if she weren't in the room.

Emma stared at the open safe from a distance, then walked over to it. As she bent over it and peered inside, she caught sight of something white gleaming softly in the darkness.

Emma reached inside. Her hand brushed against something soft, something cloth, as she drew out the mysterious white object. It was the ivory sheath. Even in the dim light, Emma knew what it was. Her hand trembled as she brought the long curved sheath out. It was cool to her touch.

She reached back inside and closed her hand around the cloth. Out of the safe, she unfolded it and gasped in horror. This was the evidence that she'd been looking for, the proof that would set Clem free. This was John's shirt, sections of it stiff with dried blood.

The door to the library creaked open. Startled, Emma looked up, dropping the shirt back in the safe and partially closing the door. She instinctively slipped the sheath between the folds of her skirt.

"Hello, Emma. I haven't seen you in a long time." He moved toward her, a dark and terrifying figure now. His face was hidden in shadows but she knew the voice. "What's that you're hiding from me?"

Emma shook her head numbly, backing away.

"You don't think that you can hide that knife sheath from me," he whispered. "I've been looking all over for it." He indicated the safe and added, "Mother must have found it and hid it in the safe. Father never gave me the combination. He didn't trust me."

He moved toward her.

CHAPTER 19

THEY rode hard, slapping leather against horseflesh to get to the Ashton ranch. Birch glanced over at his employer, noticing that Tisdale's face was a grim mask. There was no need for words between them to know what each was thinking.

Emma Johnston was heading into trouble, and the last time Birch saw her, she didn't have a gun. Even if she'd gotten hold of one, Tisdale's healing shoulder was a testament to her unfamiliarity with a shooting iron.

There was the slightest chance that John Ashton was away from the main house, maybe still out on the range for the day. But even so, Birch couldn't be sure how much Mrs. Ashton knew about her son's involvement. What lengths would she go to in order to prevent Emma from exposing John Ashton as the killer?

He dug his boot heels into Cactus's sides, hating to urge on his weary horse in such a manner but knowing that Emma's life was at stake.

The front door of the main house was open, and there was a horse tethered to the hitching post out front. Birch leapt from the saddle before Cactus had time to come to a full stop, jumped the porch steps, and knocked on the open door. Tisdale followed up the steps.

They had almost given up on anyone being in the house when a woman in black appeared. This had to be the Ashton widow. She seemed surprised and slightly puzzled that the door was open.

"Mr. Tisdale, what are you doing back here?" she asked.

Tisdale took his hat off and explained, "It was open when we knocked." He introduced Birch.

Nodding, she said to Birch, "Yes, I'm Martha Ashton, Frank's widow." Her voice cracked slightly on the last two words.

Birch was uncomfortable about talking to a woman who had just lost her husband about the possibility that her son had killed his father, but it had to be done. Emma's life was at stake.

He doffed his hat and said, "Mrs. Ashton, we're looking into your husband's murder."

She cocked her head, a wary look in her eyes, and replied, "He's already been caught. Clem Johnston is his name."

Birch nodded and said, "I know that, ma'am. That's what everyone thinks. But we just got some new information over at the Double B Ranch from Bert Baker."

Birch couldn't read her reaction. Was she scared or trying to protect someone? Mrs. Ashton reached for the door and started to close it.

Birch tried again. "Mrs. Ashton, has Emma Johnston been here recently?"

Martha Ashton remained on guard, but she paused, her expression now impassive, and said, "No, I haven't seen her at all today. Not for many weeks since this terrible tragedy. I don't think she will be coming around here much since her brother is the one accused of killing Frank."

Birch had a feeling she was lying. He took a chance and replied, "That's funny, but I could swear that's the horse she borrowed from the Baker ranch." He pointed to the unfamiliar saddled horse tied to the post.

She gasped and swiftly closed the door, but Birch's boot was faster. "Mrs. Ashton," he said forcefully, "you don't seem to understand—"

"I understand all too well," she replied with a fierceness that belied her drab appearance. "You want to blame my son for his father's death. But I saw Clem Johnston standing over my husband's body. Standing there with the knife in his hand." Tears welled up and ran down her pale cheeks.

Birch said gently, "May I ask you a question or two about what you saw in the barn? Maybe we can clear this up and a young girl's life can be saved."

She remained mute, but didn't try to close the door again.

"Who discovered Clem and your husband's body, you or John?"

"John. He didn't want me to come in, but I had to."

"Was John with you the whole morning before the murder?" She started to answer, but Birch added quickly, "Please answer truthfully. Not only Clem's life depends on it, but Emma's as well."

Her shoulders slumped and she shook her head weakly.

"I have one last question. Do you recall whether there was blood on Clem's hands and clothes?"

She looked up with resignation, her mouth quivering. Silently, she beckoned them to follow her, then turned and walked down the hall to the library. It was obvious to Birch that the room had recently been searched and for a moment, the widow looked disconcerted.

But she went over to the safe. It was ajar. She bent down and reached in without a word, pulling out a piece of cloth, a shirt. Birch touched it and shuddered. It was a shirt with dried blood on it. The widow straightened up.

"Emma must have taken the sheath," she said.

Birch grabbed her shoulders and said, "Mrs. Ashton, your son has killed once, and I'm almost certain he's going to kill Emma now. Tell me where they went."

In a near whisper, she said, "John told me that he was taking Emma out to the bunkhouse to gather her brother's things together. I heard them leave about ten minutes ago."

Birch turned to Tisdale. "Go back into Carson City and get the marshal. Ride like the devil's on your coattails."

Tisdale nodded and bustled out of the library.

The widow was swooning and he stepped to her side,

supporting her by an elbow and swiftly guiding her to a settee in the parlor.

"Please go after them, but promise me you won't hurt my son," Mrs. Ashton called to Birch as he headed out of the house.

"I can't promise anything," Birch replied grimly, "but if he gives himself up, he has nothing to worry about."

The bunkhouse door was closed. Birch went in anyway, hoping that John Ashton, a man he'd never met, was indeed only getting Clem Johnston's belongings together to give to Emma.

From the look of the place, it had been empty and dark since early morning. The stove was cold. Although clothes were scattered all over the place, one cot stood out from the others: the clothes lay in a haphazard pile, a Bowie knife, a gun, and its accompanying holster lay on top. Birch guessed that this was Clem Johnston's pile of worldly goods, waiting for someone to come and claim them.

His heart was beating a little faster as Birch left the building and looked around for a sign of where they might have gone. A small wooded area to the south of the bunkhouse caught his eye and he moved toward it. A torn piece of red calico with blue flowers had been left on a bush. Birch fingered it and looked deeper into the grove of trees, wishing he could hear them.

Realizing that Cactus would have a difficult time negotiating the close-set trees, Birch plunged into the forest on foot. He would make better time that way. He stayed with the path, running as fast as he could with the junipers tugging at his shirt whenever he had to squeeze through a narrow opening in the path.

A few minutes later, he thought he heard a sound. He stopped and listened. He heard a woman scream. It was coming from somewhere ahead of him. He ran toward the sound, but in the growing darkness of the woods, Birch stumbled and fell. When he pushed himself back up, he noticed that the low-lying brush had been severely trampled just up ahead, as if there'd been a struggle.

As he forged ahead he saw something near-white when he parted some brush. It was lying just off the path as if it had been tossed there deliberately. He reached into the bush and grasping it, held it up to the dim light of the woods—the ivory sheath! Birch tucked it into his shirt and blundered on ahead until he came to a clearing with a shallow stream.

The sound of splashing caught his attention. Emma and a strange man were thrashing around in the water. He was holding her head under and she was struggling.

Birch bounded over and grabbed the man by his collar, pulling him off her. Gasping for breath, she staggered toward the bank while the two men struggled.

Ashton tore himself away from Birch's grip. His face was twisted with rage as he lunged at Birch, his big hands trying to choke the life out of the former Ranger. Birch landed a blow to Ashton's nose, stunning him into relinquishing his hold. Ashton staggered back, started to charge Birch, then seemed to think better of it. Before Birch could do anything, John Ashton was out of the water, heading toward Emma.

Birch drew his gun just as Ashton pulled Emma in front of him. He slipped his powerful arm around Emma's neck.

"Stay away from me. This is between the woman and me," Ashton warned. "I'll kill her if I have to. I'll break her neck. Take the bullets out of your gun."

Birch had no doubt that Ashton could snap Emma's neck in a second. Young Ashton had the build of a blacksmith. Birch did as he was told.

"Throw your gun toward me," Ashton ordered. Emma whimpered and Ashton's hold tightened around her neck.

Reluctantly, Birch lowered his gun slowly and tossed it easily in Ashton's direction. It landed near the water's edge. Standing knee-deep in a stream with the sun going down was chilling Birch to the bone.

Stalling for time, he asked, "Why do you want to kill her, Ashton?"

Ashton's eyes darted around as if he were afraid someone would sneak up behind him. Although Birch could see that there was something unusual in Ashton's eyes, he couldn't put his finger on what was wrong. But he could see what Johnston meant when he'd said that John Ashton was "strange."

He answered, "She has something I want."

Birch replied, "And you'll let her go if you get it?"

Sweat beaded up above Ashton's lip. He nodded shortly and confirmed, "I'll let her go then."

Birch reached carefully into his shirt and pulled out the sheath. He held it up and asked, "Is this what you're looking for?"

John Ashton's eyes lit up, but he didn't let go of Emma. She clawed at his arm and moaned, ready to pass out from lack of air.

"Throw it over to me," Ashton commanded.

Birch knew that if he gave up the sheath, he would lose the advantage. But the stalemate wouldn't last forever. He lobbed it into the creek.

Ashton looked petulantly at Birch. "Why did you do that? Why did you throw it in there? Now I'll have to kill you both." He moved toward the creek, dragging Emma, almost unconscious, along.

Birch watched Ashton wade into the water. He knew the brook was shallow and Ashton would find the sheath in a matter of minutes. But while he hung onto Emma, he couldn't bend over and pick it up. His only alternative was to let go of her.

It didn't take long for John Ashton to find the damning evidence. Just as Birch had thought, Ashton tried to bend over, but Emma's weight had become burdensome. He let her go and she stumbled in the water.

Ashton bent over, arms submerged in the water, and tried

to get a grasp on the ivory sheath. It skidded out of his grasp and he stumbled after it. Meanwhile, Birch waded through the icy stream toward Emma and dragged her to safety on the bank.

Birch turned and dove into the creek again and tackled Ashton as he stood up, clutching the evidence. The killer wasn't ready for Birch and slipped beneath the water, struggling to regain his footing.

Birch snagged a handful of Ashton's wet shirt and pulled him up, intending to lay a right cross on him. Ashton surprised him with a rock in his hand, something he'd gotten from the creek bed, and brought it smashing down on Birch's shoulder. Pain shot through his arm and Birch loosened his grip. Ashton hit out again. This time, Birch was ready for him and dodged the blow. Moving through the water was difficult, but Ashton was having the same problems.

Birch attacked Ashton again, his right fist coming up to meet Ashton's jaw while his left found a soft spot in Ashton's gut. Ashton bent over, then collapsed in the water.

Birch hooked the back of the man's collar and pulled him out of the stream. He had nothing to tie him up with, his handcuffs having been lost somewhere between Clem Johnston's escape and Carson City.

Emma had partially recovered, although she was still coughing and breathing hard from her ordeal. Birch stripped Ashton of his shirt, twisted it into a strong rope, and used it to tie the almost unconscious man's hands behind his back.

Birch went back into the creek and looked for the sheath, keeping his eye on John Ashton in case he woke up and tried to run.

By the time he found it, Emma was standing, supported by a tall juniper. Birch couldn't tell if she was shivering from the cold or from the experience of almost being murdered.

She looked up at him, her breath still coming out in ragged gasps, her dark hair plastered against her skull.

Her eyes traveled to the still form of John Ashton.

"Is he dead?" she asked.

"No, just dazed," Birch replied.

Birch briefly searched the ground for his empty Navy Colt, found it, and put it back in his holster. He went over to John Ashton and hauled him to his feet, pushing him ahead toward the main house.

Keeping his eye on John Ashton, he took Emma's arm, and they made their way back to the Ashton ranch.

CHAPTER 20

DESPITE a shawl pulled tightly around her shoulders, Martha Ashton was shivering as she waited beside the bunkhouse for Birch, Emma, and John Ashton to emerge from the woods. She seemed to have aged ten years in the last hour.

John Ashton stumbled as he walked toward his mother, his head hanging down. His clothes were still dripping water in the cool autumn air.

She rushed up to her son and wrapped her shawl around his shoulders. Tears flowed down her cheeks as she said, "Oh, John. . . ."

John looked away, mute.

His mother touched his arm and asked, "Why, John, why?"

She seemed to know that she wouldn't get an answer, not right now. She turned away and led them into the house. After showing them into the library, she continued on to the kitchen to heat up coffee for the damp and shivering trio.

Tisdale wasn't back yet with the marshal, but Birch expected them to show up soon. With his mother out of the room, John Ashton was no longer the shamefaced boy who couldn't look his mother in the eye.

He shot a menacing look at Birch and Emma and growled, "You can't prove anything."

He still didn't know Birch's name, and Birch didn't feel much like going into introductions. He replied, "But we can prove that you tried to kill Emma, attacked me, and withheld information that the murder weapon had last been in your possession. We have your blood-soaked shirt. That's enough for a judge to question Clem Johnston's guilt and might even be enough to send you away for a few years."

Emma added, "And at least an innocent man won't be hanged for your crime."

John Ashton grinned nastily. "I'm an Ashton, though. I don't think I'll be spending more than a night or two in the local jail. I'll get out of it."

Birch looked at Ashton. There was a coldness in his eyes that warned Birch that this was a man who would kill again.

He spoke up. "Why did you kill your father?"

John Ashton turned his vacant eyes on Birch. "I'm not saying I killed him, but I had a lot of reasons to want him dead. He was unfaithful to my mother. He controlled my life. Nothing I ever did ever measured up to his standards. He was always finding something wrong with me."

Birch said, "That's still no reason to kill him."

John frowned for a moment, then continued, "The morning of his death, we got into an argument. He didn't want me to go on the next cattle drive. He said someone should stay home and look after Mother. I asked him why he didn't stay home. I could have run the cattle drive without him. But he mentioned Lily in Silver City and his other women along the trail."

Ashton's face grew darker as he spoke about his dead father. "I pulled out my knife and told him I'd kill him if he didn't agree to stop seeing those harlots. My mother deserved better."

"What did he do then?" Birch prompted.

A pained look crossed John Ashton's face as he said, "He laughed at me. Called me a mama's boy. I waved the knife to show that I meant what I said, but he started to walk past me. Then he tripped and fell on my knife." Looking up at the gathering, John fell silent.

From the doorway, Martha Ashton dropped the tray she had been carrying. She had been listening, but Birch didn't know how long she'd been there. It had been long enough. Emma got up and gently guided Mrs. Ashton to a chair, then went back and quietly picked up the tray, cups, and saucers.

"John," his mother whispered. She reached out to touch him, then turned to Birch and said, "Then it is true." She put a hand to her mouth as if to stop her lips from trembling. Emma stayed by her side, a hand on her shoulder.

His hands still tied behind his back, John looked at his mother and said, "Don't worry, Mother. Nothing's going to happen to me."

"If what you say about it being an accident is true," Birch told Ashton, "how come the doctor counted six stab wounds?"

Mrs. Ashton closed her eyes, tears continuing to slip down her cheeks. Emma comforted the widow.

John Ashton somehow had managed to work his hands free of the binding because suddenly he jumped up. He made a dash to the front door, Birch right on his heels. He opened the door and ran out into the waiting arms of the law. Tisdale had arrived with Marshal Turner. Clem Johnston was right behind them.

John Ashton sat glumly in a corner of the room while Birch, Tisdale, and Emma explained everything to Marshal Turner. As he listened, the marshal kept an impassive face.

When they had finished, he turned to Birch and said, "What I don't understand is why John brought his mother out to the barn after he had killed his father."

Mrs. Ashton had been sobbing quietly near her son. She made an effort of compose herself and spoke in a whisper. "I insisted on going out to the barn. I'd asked Frank early that morning to hitch up the horse to the buggy, but I thought he'd forgotten. Clem offered to outfit the horse-and-buggy. I went out a while later to see if it was ready. John caught me on my way out."

Sorrowfully, she looked over at her son and added, "He told me he'd take care of it and that I should go back to the house and wait, but I didn't listen." She covered her face again with her lace handkerchief.

John Ashton stared back at the group with such hate in his eyes that Birch wondered why those around him hadn't noticed that he was a troubled man before the killing.

As if she'd read his mind, Martha Ashton said gently, "I blame myself. Frank was awfully hard on John and there were plenty of times that I could have stood up for my son, but I was afraid to speak."

The marshal, his eye on John Ashton, asked, "How could he put up such a good front after killing his father?"

Tisdale answered. "I suppose when his mother walked into the barn and saw Clem with the body, it was a godsend, if you pardon the expression. Someone had to be hanged for the crime."

"After Clem escaped, John Ashton had to be sure he was recaptured," Birch added. "He didn't know how long Clem had been in the barn, how much he'd be able to put together and point the finger at him. That was why John hired Tisdale Investigations—so Clem would be spending so much time worrying about eluding a bounty hunter, he wouldn't be able to figure out who really killed Frank Ashton."

Clem Johnston spoke up for the first time. "When I was caught, John wanted the trial as soon as possible."

Turner asked another question. "Something still bothers me. How could he have had the time to kill his father, get back to the main house and change his clothes, then discover Johnston standing over the body?"

"It wasn't supposed to happen that way," Birch reminded him. "John didn't know that his mother had asked Clem Johnston to go out to the barn and hitch up the horse-and-buggy. He thought he still had time. I've never seen your barn before, Mrs. Ashton, but most barns have more than one way to get out. After killing his father, John could have slipped out a side door unseen and come straight back to the house to change his shirt."

Martha Ashton looked up from her grief. Her pained expression told Birch that he'd guessed right.

Hat in hand, Marshal Turner stood up, bringing the uncomfortable gathering to an end.

"Ma'am," he addressed the widow, "I'm afraid I'm going to have to take your son into Carson City."

Martha Ashton managed a dignified nod and watched the marshal take her handcuffed son away.

CHAPTER 21

BIRCH and Tisdale met Clem and Emma Johnston in a hotel lobby in Carson City the next morning. Emma wore a dark green wool dress, which was just right for the chilly day. Except for a few stray wisps, her wavy chestnut hair was caught up with tortoise shell combs.

Clem had taken his hat off and stood gawking at the setting. Finally, he turned his attention back to Birch and Tisdale and stuck his hand out.

"Thank you for your help, Mr. Birch," he said awkwardly. Birch shook hands gravely. Clem Johnston turned to Tisdale and said, "I hope I didn't cause you too much trouble."

Tisdale heartily shook Johnston's hand, and replied, "Not at all, my dear boy. I was along to watch and learn, and I think I've come out of this experience the wiser."

Clem Johnston nodded, a quizzical expression on his face. Birch fought back a smile.

Tisdale took Emma's hand and said, "My dear, I want you to know that I don't hold what happened during the escape against you. You're the loveliest person who has ever shot me and I'm just happy I'm alive to talk about it." He bent over her outstretched hand and lightly kissed it.

Birch and Clem Johnston roared with laughter. Emma smiled and blushed.

While Johnston and Tisdale moved away to discuss the possibility of Clem doing future work for Tisdale's agency, Emma looked up at Birch, then lowered her eyes and said, "I didn't mind it so much when you kissed me the other day."

He answered, "I enjoyed it, too."

She looked up at him. "When will you be leaving?"

He avoided her direct gaze and said, "Today."

Glancing at her, Birch noticed that Emma looked disappointed.

He added, "There's nothing keeping me here."

Emma replied, "Well, the Bakers are having another barn dance tomorrow night. And you and Mr. Tisdale are invited." She smiled and added, "We really can't thank you enough. Without your belief in Clem, he would have hanged."

"What about your faith in him? You almost died proving his innocence," Birch said.

She looked startled, as if the thought hadn't occurred to her before.

Birch changed the subject. "What will you do now?"

"Mrs. Ashton has asked me to stay on and help her around the house. And she's asked Clem to stay on as well. I think she's lonely."

Later, Tisdale collected the reward for finding Frank Ashton's killer. He split it with Birch.

Birch checked the fittings on his saddle one more time. Tisdale watched nearby.

"Do you have time for a drink, Birch?"

Birch paused and said, "You know, Mr. Tisdale, I think I'd like that."

They went into a nearby saloon and Tisdale bought a bottle. He poured a round and raised his whiskey glass to Birch.

"Here's to a long and profitable association together," Tisdale proclaimed.

Birch raised his glass in response and added firmly, "And here's to doing the job right."

They toasted and drank to each other's health, then went back outside to Birch's patiently waiting horse, Cactus.

"Where will you go next?" Tisdale wanted to know.

Birch mounted his horse and adjusted his hat as he pondered the question. He shrugged and replied, "I may stay around here for a few days. But then I suppose I'll go south. I hear there's ranch work all year round down there."

"Just wire me when you settle down. I need to know where to contact you the next time an assignment turns up."

Birch nodded. He wondered if he should give up being a Tisdale agent for something more permanent. Maybe he should buy some land and start his own ranch. He'd think about it. Meanwhile, he'd keep taking Tisdale's assignments as they were doled out—infrequently.

He wheeled Cactus around to face a southerly direction, tipped his hat to Tisdale, and rode off. Maybe he'd catch up to Emma before she got to the Ashton spread.

If you have enjoyed this book and would like to receive details of other Walker Western titles, please write to:

Western Editor
Walker and Company
720 Fifth Avenue
New York, NY 10019